Vineyard Winds

A Vineyard Sunset Series

Katie Winters

Chapter One

When Claire entered the Sunrise Cove Inn on New Year's Eve, the first thing she saw was Wes Sheridan on one knee. He raised a small velvet-lined box, his eyes glistening from the light of the Christmas tree in the foyer and presented a gorgeous engagement ring to all three of his daughters— Lola, Christine, and Susan.

"What do you think?" he said softly. "Will she like it?"

Claire was captivated. Wes Sheridan was her uncle, a man who'd lived alone for decades after the death of his wife, Anna. The fact that he'd found love again with Beatrice was beyond anyone's wildest dreams. Just last summer, he'd moved out of the Sheridan House and in with Beatrice, choosing to build a new era rather than subscribe to the rules of his previous one. He was in his seventies with early onset dementia, yet nothing had slowed him down.

"Oh, Dad." Susan took the jewelry box and inspected the ring. "It's perfect."

Wes returned to his feet and smiled sheepishly, as though he were a child who'd just presented his school project. "It took me months to decide on the ring," he explained.

"You should have asked us for help!" Susan scolded him as Lola and Christine nodded.

"You three have wonderful taste," Wes began. "But I wanted to pick it out myself. It felt more special that way."

Lola's eyes lifted toward Claire's in the doorway. "What do you think, Claire?" She tilted her head toward the ring.

Claire was slightly early for the New Year's Eve party. In her arms were heaps of flowers she'd brought from the flower shop, which she'd owned and operated for decades. Her plan was to decorate the Sunrise Cove Bistro before the guests arrived. She hadn't imagined she'd walk into such a tremendously poignant moment.

"I'm so sorry for interrupting," Claire stammered.

"Don't you worry about that." Uncle Wes smiled warmly and beckoned for Claire to come closer.

Claire placed the flowers on the front desk of the inn and peered at the diamond ring, which had been exquisitely cut. Uncle Wes explained it was vintage, made in 1917 for a man whose fiancée had nearly died on the *Titanic* as a girl. He'd wanted a ring that captured the fantastical reality of her life. "She never thought she should have survived," Wes explained as he pocketed the jewelry box. "And she never was able to be convinced otherwise, despite living until she was one hundred and two years old."

"When are you going to ask Beatrice?" Claire asked.

"Around midnight," Uncle Wes said. "I don't want to

do it in front of everyone. Beatrice isn't the kind of gal who wants an audience for something so intimate. Besides. Who knows? She might say no." He stuttered slightly as though he was genuinely nervous.

"Why would she say no to you, Dad?" Lola teased. "You have a perfect life together."

The front door burst open, bringing a gush of chilly air and two more Sheridan women— Amanda, who was so pregnant that she had a slight waddle, and Audrey, who carried her two-and-a-half-year-old son, Max. The girls were dressed immaculately: Audrey in a little black dress with a fur coat over it and Amanda in a riveting, sparkly dress. Both wore bright red lipstick, and their dark curls cascaded down their backs.

"Grandpa!" Audrey exclaimed. "What do you have there?"

Wes's eyes sparkled knowingly as he passed the jewelry box to his granddaughters. Claire remained captivated, her heart in her throat. A very long time ago, her husband, Russel, had gotten down on one knee and asked her to pledge his life to her. It had felt like a moment frozen in time: his eyes glistening from the fading sunset over the Vineyard Sound, Claire's skin dry from swimming all day, their entire lives stretching out in front of them.

More and more of the Montgomery and Sheridan family members breezed through the doors of the Sunrise Cove. In the chaos, Claire stepped away to decorate the bistro with flowers, taking special care along the bar top and in the corners. Zach, Christine's husband and the chef of the bistro, stepped out from the kitchen to say hello, drying his hands on his apron.

"You're working hard," he said.

"I just want the place to look nice," Claire said. "I hope you're not cooking all night?"

"Everything is prepped," Zach assured her. "I'll be taking off these chef whites here in a second."

Claire beamed and gestured toward the crowd in the foyer. "Did you hear? Wes is going to propose."

Zach shook his head. "Imagine starting over at that age?"

Claire chuckled. "It gives me hope, in a way. He's thirty years older than I am. There's still so much life to live."

Just then, Charlotte broke through the crowd in the foyer and hurried down toward the bistro, her arms outstretched.

"There you are! I thought I told you to wait for me at the flower shop so I could help?" Charlotte wrapped her arms around Claire. "You're too impatient for your own good."

Claire closed her eyes and allowed herself a moment of joy in the arms of her best friend and sister, Charlotte. At the end of summer, Charlotte moved west to Orcas Island with her fiancé, Everett. Claire had begun to feel them drifting apart despite weekly phone calls and daily texting. Charlotte was falling in love with a new island and gorgeous, different views, leaving Claire alone on Martha's Vineyard to tend to their parents and the flower shop. Even her daughters, Gail and Abby, had gone to university off the island.

The truth was that it had been the loneliest few months of Claire's life. But she hadn't admitted it to anyone yet. She was in denial, thinking it would probably change soon. That everything would get better.

"Where's Russel?" Charlotte asked, glancing back toward the crowded foyer.

"Gail, Abby, and Russel should be on their way." Claire had left them in a quiet house, Gail and Abby in their separate bedrooms and Russel in the computer room, tending to their stocks.

"You're taking the girls back on the fifth?"

Claire nodded. "I tried to bribe them into staying a little bit longer. They told me some baloney about needing to attend their college classes in order to graduate."

"Isn't it terrible? We should have forbidden our girls from growing up when we had the chance," Charlotte said.

Zach burst from the kitchen doors. He'd changed out of his chef whites and into a pair of dark jeans and a black turtleneck, and he scouted through the throng of Montgomerys and Sheridans to find his wife, Christine. Christine had their baby, Mia, in her arms, and Zach knelt to kiss Mia gently on the cheek. Claire had a memory of Russel and her girls when they were that small. He'd carried them both at once, one nestled gently in each of his arms, and walked up and down the hallway until they'd fallen asleep. Claire had called him the baby whisperer.

The Sheridans had hired bartenders for the New Year's Eve party. They were dressed in little tuxedos and scouting through the guests, asking for drink orders or passing out champagne. Charlotte and Claire both took flutes and clinked them together.

"Remember when we used to drink sparkling apple juice on New Year's?" Charlotte said.

"I remember pretending to be tipsy," Claire said, "and giggling so much that Dad yelled down the hall for us to be quiet."

Charlotte sipped her champagne contemplatively. Claire had the urge to ask if Charlotte was happy out there on Orcas Island and if it was worth moving so far away from home. Was her love for Everett really that strong?

Then again, Claire worried that if she said something like that, Charlotte would see the holes within Claire's own life. Maybe she would ask: don't you believe in love anymore?

And Claire would be forced to reckon with that question. She wasn't sure she was strong enough.

"Look! Rina's back." Charlotte bowed her head toward the slender woman with a brunette bob, who clutched a glass of champagne nervously and stayed close to Steve, their older brother.

"What did she say at Thanksgiving?" Claire tried to remember. "Something about going to Oaxaca?"

"I think she had a case down there," Charlotte said. "Steve said she found who she was looking for. Some husband who'd decided to run out on his kids again. But I didn't know she was coming back."

Rina was a private investigator from California. Last spring, she'd come to Martha's Vineyard to look for a young woman who'd disappeared. Steve and his daughter, Isabella, had eventually helped her crack the case and bring the young woman home. Despite clear attraction between Steve and Rina, it wasn't clear to the rest of the family if they'd made anything official. Steve had lost his wife, Laura, in September of 2022— a little less than a year and a half ago. He remained in grief therapy. He and his family continued to reel.

"She's patient," Claire affirmed. "Waiting for Steve for so long like that."

"Steve's special," Charlotte muttered. "Of course, he's mum on the subject. Andy pestered him for information about their relationship, and he just grunted and walked away."

"Typical Steve," Claire said. "He's just like Dad."

A second later, Gail's voice shot through the crowd. Claire went on high alert, knowing her daughter was in distress.

"Won't you cut it out?" Gail rasped angrily. "I told you. I don't want to talk about it."

Claire and Charlotte exchanged worried glances. Claire slipped through the crowd, between Andy's wife, Beth and Christine and Susan, to find Gail, Abby, and Rachel near a long table of hors d'oeuvres. It wasn't surprising that the three of them were together. Since birth, Charlotte's daughter, Rachel, had been sort-of a stand-in triplet. They'd had what felt like thousands of sleepovers, birthday parties, beach days, hikes, spontaneous dance parties, and sing-alongs.

But now, Gail's cheeks were cherry red, and she glared at Rachel and Abby, her arms tightly crossed over her chest. Claire had never seen her daughter look at her twin and cousin like this.

"Hey, girls?" Claire said, forcing all three pairs of eyes toward her. "Did you just get here?"

Gail's shoulders slumped forward. While Rachel and Abby were in sparkly dresses, Gail wore a pair of ratty jeans and a black sweatshirt. She'd lined her eyes with thick charcoal as though she'd just stepped out of a goth music video.

Rachel wore an uneasy smile. "Happy New Year, Aunt Claire."

Gail huffed, turned on her heel, and shot through the crowd, heading toward the foyer. Claire watched her go, her heart pounding in her throat.

"Is Gail feeling all right?" Charlotte asked.

Rachel and Abby exchanged a mysterious glance. Together, the three of them had a silent language that Claire and Charlotte didn't understand.

"She's okay," Abby stuttered. "It's just been a weird day."

Rachel nodded furiously. It was clear they were covering something up.

"Come on, girls," Claire pressed it. "Let's not start the new year off like this. What's going on? Charlotte and I can help."

Suddenly, a large, strong hand pressed against Claire's lower back. Russel's lips found Claire's cheek for a scratchy kiss. "Happy New Year's Eve, honey," Russel said.

Claire turned into Russel's warmth, surprised at how intimate he was with her. It had been a few days since they'd touched—and a few weeks or months since they'd slept together. It was an immediate distraction from the teenage drama in front of her.

"Happy New Year's Eve!" Claire echoed, smiling at Russel. "Thanks for bringing the girls."

"No problem," Russel said.

Abby and Rachel disappeared back through the crowd, snaking away from Claire and Charlotte, whispering in one another's ears.

"Were they fighting before you left?" Claire asked.

Russel furrowed his brow. His arm was still slung around Claire's waist, and she dropped her head against his shoulder. The champagne made her bubbly; it made the warmth and happiness around her feel surreal.

"They seemed normal on the drive," Russel said.

"They're eighteen," Charlotte said with a shrug. "It's not up to us to understand everything they're going through."

"I've never heard Gail talk to Abby like that," Claire offered.

Russel laughed and shook his head. "They're mostly out of our jurisdiction these days," he said. "Who knows what they're getting up to in college? They're becoming their own people. Sometimes, I wonder if it was a mistake to let them live in the same dorm room together."

Charlotte sipped her champagne, considering this. "But they insisted on it, right?"

"We can't split them up," Claire said, feeling a wave of fear. Gail and Abby had always been inseparable. Gail had been born first, but Abby followed just a second afterward, as though she didn't want Gail to be lonely.

"But they'll split up eventually," Russel reminded her. "They'll get older, have different jobs, and marry different men. They'll have different families. Different opinions, even!" Russel's tone was sarcastic, but his smile was endearing, drawing Claire closer.

"Maybe they can marry twin guys and all live together in a big house," Charlotte joked. "And maybe Rachel can live with her husband next door." Clearly, Charlotte had noticed Claire's fears and wanted to calm her.

Claire sighed and finished the rest of her glass of

champagne. It was time for another; it was time to fall into the gorgeous night and celebrate with her family. Russel was probably right that her girls were just going through growing pains. They were just trying to make sense of being eighteen and on the brink of the rest of their lives. Claire had been young once. She remembered.

Chapter Two

The downstairs bathroom of the Sunrise Cove Inn had an enormous, gold-plated mirror that hung from the ceiling to the floor. It looked like something from the deep past—1920s Paris or Rome, and it was difficult to imagine any Sheridan member ever picking it out. Had it been a selection of Anna Sheridan? The mother who'd died so long ago? Even for Rina, a private investigator accustomed to puzzles and problems, it was hard to make sense of this family, with its numerous secrets and past lives. Rina inspected her reflection in the antique mirror, twisting her torso, looking at her short yet slender legs, her flat feet, and the small belly she'd developed over the holidays. It was nice to take this moment alone in the bathroom and hide from the questioning eyes of the Sheridans and Montgomerys as they celebrated deeper into the night.

Rina knew what they wanted to know. Were Rina and Steve "together" yet? Had Steve actually moved on after his wife's death? And if he hadn't, what was Rina doing here, hanging around so many months after last spring's case had closed? Was she just pathetic?

Rina wasn't entirely sure how to answer that question, even unto herself. Her entire body ached with sorrow and loneliness when she was in California. While on Martha's Vineyard, she felt soft and pliable; she laughed often and opened her heart in ways she'd forgotten were possible. And she told herself that the timeline of her "will they, won't they" romance with Steve was nobody else's business but hers and Steve's. And she tried not to allow herself to break her own heart.

Of course, Rina understood Steve's hesitation. He'd lost his life partner. With Laura gone, he had to unravel decades of memories and make sense of himself in the world alone. His children had tried to follow his lead, but they were often just as lost as he was.

The bathroom door flew open. Three teenage girls entered, two of them in dresses and the other in black jeans. Their names were Gail, Abby, and Rachel— twins and a cousin. Although Rina had met all of the Montgomery family members, she was generally terrified of the younger ones. Teenage girls could be cruel.

It was then she realized Gail was crying. Fat tears rolled down her cheeks, bringing the black charcoal from her eyes to her chin. Just when Rina prepared to ask what was wrong, Gail gave her a scathing glare that meant she wanted privacy.

"You girls tell me if you need anything," Rina murmured, hurrying past and re-entering the hall.

"There she is." Steve's voice swelled from the right, and Rina turned as he approached with a glass of champagne. His smile was boyish, proof he'd had a few drinks already. "Come on," he said. "They're playing games in the bistro."

Rina followed Steve through the crowd and took a seat across from Trevor, Kerry, and Kelli, Steve's father, mother, and sister. Soon after, Steve's cousin, Lola, appeared and dropped into the seat beside her, flashing her long hair behind her shoulders. Steve shuffled a deck of cards and passed them out as Lola and Trevor made small talk and lightly gossiped about members of their family. Just then, Rina spotted Uncle Wes moving through the crowd, holding Beatrice's hand, and Lola turned to whisper in Rina's ear.

"My dad's going to propose tonight," she said. "I'm terrified!"

It was rare that Rina felt drawn so deeply into the secrets of this family. "Do you think she'll say yes?"

Lola raised her shoulders. "I don't know. I hope so. My father needs a win, I think. Gosh, she looks beautiful tonight, doesn't she? I hope I look half as good in my sixties."

It was difficult for Rina to imagine Lola looking anything but stunning. The Sheridan women all looked nearly identical to their late mother, Anna, who'd been a knock-out. Steve had explained the heartbreaking story of Anna's death, that she'd been having an affair with a man who'd accidentally drowned her.

"Were you ever married, Rina?" Trevor asked spontaneously.

Rina was startled at the forward question. Steve's cheeks were pale.

"I was," Rina said, her voice wavering. She'd told Steve all about Vic many months ago—that she'd been head-over-heels for him and had married him in her twenties. They'd tried for children that hadn't come, and ultimately, Vic had cheated on her and broken up with her shortly thereafter. But she wasn't sure she wanted to get into it with Trevor Montgomery on New Year's Eve. It wasn't a story she generally liked to tell.

"Plenty of people were married," Kelli said, waving her hand. "I was married to the world's most horrific man."

"And now, you're engaged to a wonderful man," Trevor said, punching Kelli lightly on the arm. "Where is Xander? Is he around here somewhere?"

Rina and Steve locked eyes over the table. Rina breathed a sigh of relief. Trevor had forgotten his question just as soon as Kelli had distracted him.

"Rina," Lola interjected. "Tell us about your recent gig in Oaxaca! Did you find the guy? The one who disappeared?"

Everyone was always intrigued by Rina's work. There was something about finding people who'd "disappeared" that captured everyone's imagination. But for Rina, her job often left her with a feeling of sorrow about humanity. People abandoned people, unwilling to offer the support they'd once promised. She'd seen so many holes within families that she'd begun to doubt anyone was actually "good" deep down.

Except Steve. She genuinely couldn't find anything wrong with him.

"She found him in ten days flat," Steve bragged of Rina. "I remember over the phone that you told me you thought it would be complicated. You thought you were going to have to live in Oaxaca for a while and work the case."

Rina felt a wave of relief. "I got lucky with that one,"

she said. "The guy had abandoned his wife and children in Oklahoma, and the wife really needed help. She couldn't pay for food, and they were going to lose the house." Rina recited a very common story in the United States and among her clients. "When I got to Oaxaca, the trail went cold until I happened to meet with a young woman in her twenties whose sister had just fallen in love with 'some American guy.'" Rina used air quotes, remembering that sunny day on the coast. "She hated her sister's new boyfriend so much. She would have done anything to get him out of their hair. And it just so happened he was the guy I was looking for."

Everyone at the table laughed. Trevor's eyes sparkled.

"You're quite impressive, Rina," Trevor said. "No doubt about that."

Suddenly, an uproar of celebration came from the other side of the room. Wes and Beatrice were in the doorway, their hands linked and raised over their heads. Beatrice's eyes glinted with tears, and Wes's smile was enormous, extending his crow's feet from his eyes to his hairline.

"Oh my gosh! It happened!" Lola whipped up from the table and hurried through the crowd to hug Beatrice first and then Wes. "It's gorgeous, Dad," Lola said, both hands around Beatrice's left one as she gazed at the ring. "You know, he picked this out all by himself? He didn't want any help from us girls."

Under the table, Steve took Rina's hand and squeezed it just once, then let it go. Rina's heart flipped over. She immediately stood, excused herself, and retreated to the backyard, where she stood without a coat, breathing in and out and filling the air before her with steam. Just a few feet away, the Vineyard Sound lapped up onto the beach, and the froth caught the light of the low-hanging moon. Beyond that, the water was inky black and impossibly deep.

To Rina, the ocean was different on this side of the continent. It was angrier. It told different stories. Here near Martha's Vineyard, it had swallowed up so many whalers and fishermen. Even in the Montgomery and Sheridan families, it had drowned Charlotte's first husband and Wes's first wife.

Again, Rina heard a rasp and words of anger coming from the other side of the inn. If she wasn't mistaken, it was the teenagers again—Gail, Abby, and Rachel.

"I don't want your help," one of them was saying. "I want you to leave me alone for a change. Do you understand?"

"Gail," the other wailed. "Please. Help me understand."

Rina ducked away from the inn, not wanting to eavesdrop on their teenage drama. You were allowed so little privacy at that age. She didn't want to destroy it.

As she walked through the cold, her head stirred with questions. When Steve touched her, her heart ballooned in her chest, making it difficult to breathe. Sometimes, when she came to visit, they fell asleep next to one another as they talked deep into the night. Sometimes, Steve fell asleep midsentence and woke up the following morning, prepared to dive back into the same conversation.

A long time ago, when Vic left her, Rina promised herself she wouldn't fall in love again. Her mission in life was her work.

Yet here she was. Wasting time. Hadn't she turned

down a potential gig just because she'd wanted to come out East and spend time with Steve? She could hardly recognize herself anymore.

It was terribly cold, with a ten-degree windchill. The fact that she traipsed around the inn without a coat was more proof of her insanity. From outside, she could peer through the window of the Bistro and watch the Montgomery and Sheridan celebration and feel the buzzing of their laughter through the walls. How was it they were able to find such joy in their everyday lives? Had they figured something out about the world that others hadn't?

Nearest the window was Rina's favorite couple, Isabella and Rhett, who'd begun their romance when Rina first came to the island. Initially, Rina had suspected Rhett of being involved with a crime. He'd even briefly gone to jail. But upon his release, he'd stopped at nothing to prove his innocence and save the young woman—and even gotten hurt in the process.

Since then, he and Isabella had fallen deeper in love. And because Rina was so often around, she'd been allowed a front-row seat. She and Steve had often discussed this abstractly, referring to what it had first felt like for them to fall in love. During these conversations, Rina knew Steve referred to Laura, his wife, although he didn't mention her by name. Always, Rina was talking about her teenage boyfriend, Cody, who'd had legs too long for his body and shaggy blond hair. She'd broken up with him when she'd gotten into college and he'd decided to go to Europe to meet his grandparents. They'd communicated via letters for a while—holding on to a childish hope of romance that they eventually watched fade.

Rina hoped for better when it came to Isabella and

Rhett. She hoped she'd have the privilege of being at their wedding one day.

Rina's phone buzzed in her pocket, interrupting her reverie. It was her father, calling from California. A shiver of fear raced down her spine. Rina hadn't spoken to either of her parents in months—not since the previous summer when words that couldn't be taken back had been exchanged. Nobody knew this, not even Steve. Rina had often considered her trips out East to be running away from her problems at home.

"Dad?" Rina answered, unable to conceal her surprise.

"Rina." Her father's voice was ragged and older than she remembered. "Rina, something has happened."

Rina could no longer feel the harsh wind against her face. She could no longer hear the vibrant celebrations within the bistro. It was as though her consciousness had whittled down to only the sound of her father's voice, all the way across the continent.

"Your mother," he explained. "There was an accident. They don't know if she's going to make it."

* * *

Rina burst back through the foyer of the Sunrise Cove. From the bistro came the sound of someone singing—was it Lola? Kelli? Rina couldn't tell, especially not through the cacophony of the other Sheridans and Montgomerys speaking over one another. Rina was scattered and out of her mind with worry. The sharp chill outside was a horrible reminder of how far away from home she was, how nothing in her life had gone as she'd originally planned. She had to get out of there.

Rina returned to the bathroom to clean herself up. Outside, tears had sprung and frozen on her cheeks, and she rubbed her face with hot water, trying and failing to come up with a plan. What could she tell Steve? She'd never told him what had happened with her family back in California. Whenever she'd spoken about her parents, she'd mentioned them within the context of her childhood —not her adulthood. She'd spoken of them as though they were fictional characters in a book.

The bathroom door burst open yet again to reveal Gail, the twin in jeans and a black sweatshirt who'd been crying. Rina blinked at her in the mirror, waiting for Gail's twin to appear immediately afterward. But it seemed Gail was alone. Rina had never seen them apart before.

Gail set her jaw and stormed toward the mirror, where she procured eyeliner from her pocket and drew thick lines around her eyes. Rina could see herself in this anger. She remembered herself as a wild and brash teenager who'd listened to punk music too loudly in her car and whipped down Highway 1—ready to take on the world. Or escape it. One or the other.

"Do you want some lipstick?" Rina surprised herself.

Gail blinked at her confusedly. Her lips were slightly chapped; dead skin hung in awkward places. "Okay," she said.

Rina dug her bright red lipstick from her purse and handed it over to Gail, who tapped at her lips nervously. Rina felt on the verge of weeping, remembering how foolish she'd been with makeup as a teenager. Remembering how she'd asked her mother to help her, but her mother had never gotten around to it.

Now, Rina fought the urge to offer her assistance

because Gail didn't want it. Gail wanted to do everything alone.

Gail did the best she could with the lipstick. It smeared out of line in certain spots, and the color was slightly too garish on her. Gail was a pale redhead, while Rina was a tan California brunette. Still, a certain camaraderie existed when exchanging beauty supplies in the bathroom. Rina had wanted a child so badly when she'd been married to Vic; would she have had moments like this with her daughter? Would she have had good instincts?

"Why are you crying?" Gail asked. Her sharp tone was proof of her inner rage.

Rina wasn't sure what to say. "I just got some terrible news."

Gail furrowed her brow and passed the lipstick back. "Join the club. I guess it's just one of those nights, huh?" She said it as though she'd been through the wringer. "What are you going to do about it?"

Rina drifted toward the mirror and put on the lipstick expertly. "I have to go home," she said.

"Isn't that in California?"

Rina nodded. "That's where I technically live. And it's where my parents are."

"I've always wanted to go to California," Gail said. Her hard edges began to melt. "What part?"

"Los Angeles," Rina said. "I grew up in Santa Monica. By the ocean."

"Just like me."

"It's a very different ocean," Rina said. "But yes, I can't imagine living far from water."

"Try living in Amherst."

"Is that where you're going to college?"

Gail nodded and rubbed her temples. Her eyes were distant. In Rina's pocket, her phone began to buzz again. It was her father. He wavered with uncertainty, so far away. And for once, he needed Rina.

"What bad news did you get tonight?" Rina asked, gripping her phone, daring herself to stay in this bathroom a little longer with this young woman who clearly needed her.

Gail forced her eyes toward Rina's. "News that changes everything." With that, she turned on her heel, smashed the flats of her palms against the door, and stormed out of the bathroom. Rina's ears rang with her boots stomping along the hardwood floor.

Chapter Three

Claire, Russel, Gail, and Abby clambered into the family van at one in the morning on the first day of 2024. Claire had drunk a few too many glasses of champagne, and her ears still rang from the celebration they'd left behind at the Sunrise Cove. Effervescent from their engagement, Wes and Beatrice were still pouring champagne inside, Susan and Scott ballroom danced, and even Amanda, who was normally the more conscientious of the Sheridans, was still awake, her arm slung around her husband Sam's waist.

"It was a great party." Claire glanced back toward Gail and Abby, who remained quiet. Had this been any other year, it would have been loud and raucous back there, with the twins gossiping about what had happened that night, the "bad fashion" they'd seen family members wearing, or the ridiculous stories their grandpa Trevor had told them. But Gail stared out the window, her arms crossed firmly over her chest. Abby looked at Gail, confusion etched across her face.

"Didn't you think it was a fabulous party?" Claire pushed it. "Abby? Did you try the salmon puffs?"

Abby jumped and forced her eyes to her mother. "Um? I didn't."

Russel touched Claire's thigh as he drove them safely back home. "They're tired," he said softly. "It's only been an hour long, but it's been a hard year so far."

Russel pulled into the driveway as the garage door yawned open and swallowed the van whole. Even before he cut the engine, Gail jumped out and hurried inside. Abby scampered after her, leaving Claire and Russel alone in the van. Claire's heart pounded with nerves.

"They're just having a bad night," Russel said again, lacing his fingers through Claire's.

"I just hate the look on Gail's face," Claire murmured. "She looks like she's in so much pain." She turned to gaze at Russel, whom she'd kissed at midnight for the twenty-fifth year in a row. "Do you think it's a guy? Maybe someone at college?"

"Honestly, it could be anything," Russel said. "Let's have a nightcap upstairs and hit the hay. Everything will be brighter in the morning."

But things weren't brighter the following morning, nor any of the ones after that. There was an icy quality to the air in Claire's house, one that made her inclined to tiptoe around to avoid reproachful glances from her twins. It didn't seem so long ago that the three of them had watched rom-coms and painted their toenails and fingernails, laughing at the silly decisions of the characters on-screen. "That is so unrealistic," Gail had said of *Serendipity*, the John Cusack and Kate Beckinsale film that believed in the power of destiny. And Abby and Claire had giggled and agreed.

Now, the twins refused to eat at the table with Claire and Russel. They kept to their separate rooms, with Gail playing music louder than she ever had. The floorboards rattled.

Once, Claire got up the nerve to demand that everyone eat at the dining room table "as a family." Abby and Russel sat in their normal chairs, staring at Gail's empty one as the food got colder and colder. Claire stomped upstairs, anger brimming, and told Gail through the door that if she didn't come downstairs, she couldn't eat at all. Gail called back, "Don't care!" And that broke Claire's heart even more. Ultimately, she caved and brought Gail a plate around nine-thirty, unable to let her daughter go hungry. To Charlotte, she texted:

> Maybe I'm weak? I just don't know what
> to do.

On the night before Claire planned to drive Gail and Abby back to the University of Massachusetts, Charlotte and Rachel swung by with take-out quesadillas, tacos, and chimichangas. Rachel looked stricken, her eyes to the ceiling as Gail played angry punk music upstairs.

"Can I go upstairs, Aunt Claire?" Rachel asked nervously.

"Why don't you take Gail's and Abby's food up with you?" Claire suggested. She knew the twins would refuse to come downstairs. Her private hope was that Rachel would knock some sense into them.

As soon as Rachel disappeared upstairs, Claire crumpled into Charlotte. "They've hardly spoken at all since New Year's Eve."

"Oh, no." Charlotte sighed and poured them both glasses of wine from a bottle of Cab she'd brought over. "I guess tomorrow they'll be forced to deal with each other. They live in the same dorm room, for crying out loud."

"It makes me really sad that they can't deal with their problems here," Claire said softly. "We get so little time as a family these days. I imagined a cozy time together, eating chocolate and watching movies."

"It's hard to translate to teenagers how precious time is," Charlotte agreed. "Rachel spent all afternoon yesterday video chatting with some boy she likes from college. I wanted to go shopping! I wanted to have those soul-affirming conversations you're supposed to have as daughters and mothers!"

Claire tried to laugh this off. She removed a tortilla chip from the paper bag and dipped it in queso. Upstairs, Gail turned the music down. Maybe Rachel was begging her to listen to reason. Maybe everything would be okay.

"I meant to ask you," Charlotte said, snapping her fingers. "What did you think of Rina running out of the party the other night?"

Claire dug through her champagne-laced memories. Not long before midnight, Rina had walked into the bistro with her coat on, whispered something in Steve's ear, hugged him, and then darted out without saying goodbye to anyone else. Nobody had been brave enough to ask Steve what was going on.

"Do you think she ended things with Steve?" Claire asked. "Just like that?"

"We don't even know if anything was happening between them."

Claire bit her lower lip. "Steve isn't talking to you about it anymore?"

Because Charlotte had lost Jason in a fishing accident, Steve had leaned heavily on her after Laura's death, asking her for guidance as he waded through the murky depths of being a widower.

"We haven't been as close since I left." Charlotte sighed. She put down her glass of wine and reached across the table to touch Claire's hand. "And I know we've been a little bit distant, too. I want to get better about that."

"You've been busy. You're building a new life. I know that."

"That doesn't mean I want to lose touch with my life here," Charlotte said. "You're my best friend, Claire. You're my sister. Nothing can get in the way of that."

* * *

The following morning, Claire gave herself a pep talk in the bathroom mirror. "They're your daughters. You gave birth to them. Talk to them. Figure this out."

Russel had already gone off to work. He'd left a half pot of coffee and a note to Gail and Abby wishing them good luck on their second semester. Abby read it as she sipped her coffee and smiled sadly to herself. When Gail clunked down the stairs, her shoulders sagging from her backpack, she took one look at the note, crumpled it in her fist, and threw it in the trash.

"Gail!" Claire cried.

Gail didn't respond and instead poured herself a mug of coffee and glowered out the window, where a soft snow spun from the low gray clouds. "I'm ready to get out of here," she said.

Claire thought something she never thought she would—that she couldn't wait for Gail to be gone, too. The thought stunned her into silence. To busy herself, she carried Abby's bag to the van, donned her coat, and got into the driver's seat to wait for the twins. They walked out of the house a minute later, Gail first, then Abby a few seconds later. "Here we go," Claire muttered to herself.

The drive was uneventful. Abby and Gail were quiet as usual, looking out opposite windows as Claire drove and listened to the radio. Sometimes, she sang along with a song, hoping one would chime in like they used to.

The drive from Woods Hole to Amherst lasted two hours and forty-five minutes. When Claire pulled onto campus, she found herself in line with another fifty or so parents, dropping off their children after Christmas break. On the sidewalk, mothers and fathers hugged their children goodbye with tears in their eyes.

"Just drop us off in front," Gail said.

"I thought I could find a spot," Claire said, her voice breaking. "Maybe we could have lunch together?"

"I'm not hungry," Gail said.

"Abby?" Claire asked. "We could go? Just us?"

Abby sighed into her hands. "Okay."

It was surreal watching Gail stomp into the dorms without Abby. Claire gripped the steering wheel, feeling like she'd just let Gail into the big, bad world without assistance. She remained quiet for the next five minutes, hunting around campus for a parking spot. But when she and Abby clambered out and strode toward Antonio's Pizza, Abby's favorite, Claire finally burst. "Abby. You have to tell me what's going on."

Abby stared at her feet as they walked. She looked as forlorn as Gail looked angry. "I don't know."

"I don't believe you," Claire said. "You and Gail have

always told each other everything. She must have mentioned what's going on."

Abby glared at Claire. "Things change, Mom."

Claire ordered a spinach and feta pizza with black olives at the pizza restaurant, and Abby ordered a pepperoni and mushroom. Midway through their meal, Claire waved to the server and asked to order another pizza—anchovies and onions, for Gail. She would force Abby to take it into the dorm room for her. Gail would be hungry later.

"If your sister ever reveals what's going on," Claire began as she cleaned her hands with a napkin, "will you let me know?"

Abby raised her shoulders. "It's private."

"But if Gail is in danger, I need to know," Claire reminded her. "If something is medically wrong with her, I need to know. If she's depressed—"

"I get it," Abby said.

Claire stared down at the greasy remains of her pizza, no longer hungry. Parenting had been so easy until now. She'd laughed at other parents of teenagers who'd struggled with their tempers in the face of haughty teenagers.

"And are you doing okay?" Claire asked.

"I'm fine."

Claire sighed. "You'd tell me if something was up, right? If you're sick or feeling sad."

"I guess."

This conversation was going nowhere. Claire was exhausted. She just wanted to drop Abby off, drive back home, and curl up in bed with a good book. She wanted Russel to take her in his arms and remind her that this was just a phase. Even the bizarreness between Russel and Claire just now was a phase that often made Claire feel like she had two heads. It was rare for them to reach for one another; their kisses and conversations were fewer and farther between. Perhaps they just needed to put the spark back in their marriage. A vacation could help. A romantic dinner out.

At the door to the dormitory, Claire hugged Abby close and said, "Make sure Gail gets her pizza."

"Okay." Abby's eyes were difficult to read.

"And make sure you tell her I love her," Claire said. "I love you, too, Abby. So much."

"I love you, too."

When Claire got back to Martha's Vineyard around five, Russel texted to say he'd be home late. Just as she'd promised herself she would, Claire put on her pajamas and curled up under the blankets, ready to fall away from the world. Before she did, she decided to text Abby.

> CLAIRE: Did you give your sister the pizza?

> ABBY: It's in the mini-fridge. She isn't here.

> CLAIRE: Did she leave a note about where she was going?

> ABBY: No.

Something stirred in Claire's gut. It felt like intuition. Something was off.

But a moment later, Abby texted.

> ABBY: It's not weird or anything.

> ABBY: Maybe she just went to the dining hall.

CLAIRE: Will you let me know when she
gets back?

ABBY: Okay.

Claire turned on *The Crown* and tried to fall into rhythm with members of the British royalty; she tried to appreciate the lush halls and beautiful clothing. But more often than not, her mind returned to thoughts of Gail. Three hours later, Abby still hadn't texted to say Gail was back. Where could she be?

Claire texted Charlotte for help.

CHARLOTTE: Maybe this is more proof
that whatever is going on has nothing to
do with you?

CHARLOTTE: Maybe she's fighting with a
boyfriend somewhere.

CHARLOTTE: Or maybe she's with a new
group of friends she doesn't share with
Abby.

Russel returned home around eleven thirty with dark circles beneath his eyes. He undressed and clambered into bed beside Claire, gesturing vaguely toward the television. "Can you turn that off, please?"

Claire hadn't realized *The Crown* was still playing. "Gail never came back to her dorm room tonight."

"It's still early," Russel said. "She's eighteen years old. She probably goes to sleep around three or four."

Claire propped herself up on three pillows. She hadn't eaten since lunch, and she felt jittery and sick to her stomach. "Is that supposed to make me feel better?"

Russel rolled his eyes just a bit and placed his hand on her thigh. It was cold as bone. "We were never helicopter parents, Claire. We always prided ourselves on that. Remember? We always made fun of the other parents for worrying too much."

"The girls never gave us reason to worry," Claire barked.

Russel looked very tired. The light from the television gave his face a ghoulish tint. "Why don't you try to sleep? Things will look brighter tomorrow. And I guarantee that by the next time you see Gail, she'll be totally over whatever this is. I can't guarantee she won't be upset about something else by then. But like I said, she's eighteen. She's going through tons of stuff right now. We have to give her space."

It didn't take long for Russel to fall asleep that night. Claire remained upright, pressing against the pillows as her heart raced in overdrive. She closed her eyes and tried to visualize Gail—tried to imagine her in a friend's dorm, maybe drinking a beer or laughing at a YouTube video. Maybe she was doing something completely normal.

But the problem was that Claire couldn't imagine Gail anywhere. It was as though there was a black hole where her motherly instincts should have been. It terrified her. And it wasn't until four or five in the morning, as winter birds twittered on the tree branches outside, that Claire grabbed any sleep. All the while, Russel slept like a log.

Chapter Four

The first case Rina had ever tried to solve, she'd failed. She still felt the sorrow of that failure in every part of her body—in the ache of her shoulders and the strain of her beating heart. Even now, as she traced the Los Angeles highways toward Santa Monica, she could remember what it had felt like on the day she'd officially "given up the search" for the missing girl. It had been like chopping up her soul into tiny pieces. It had been like acknowledging that the world could be a very dark and horrible place. As a teenager from sunny Santa Monica, this had never occurred to her. It shaped the way she'd encountered everyone for the rest of her life.

But the missing girl hadn't just been anyone; she'd been Penny, her sister. This was another thing Rina had never told Steve about. "My sister went missing when she was fifteen" didn't flow naturally over burritos and margaritas. Besides, hadn't Rina done her best to shove her sister's memory as deep into the belly of her soul as she could? Penny had been her best friend, an extension of herself. And then, one afternoon after school, Rina had stayed late to work on a paper with a boy she'd liked—and Penny had walked home alone. She'd never made it.

At the Santa Monica Pier, Rina miraculously found parking and stepped out onto the sands. The Pacific Ocean lapped gently along the beach, and the Ferris wheel circled overhead, churning its tourists through the cotton-candy blue sky.

Rina had several missed calls and texts from Steve. It wasn't like them to go more than a day or two without speaking. But she'd left in a wild rush on New Year's Day without an explanation, and he'd been staggering with confusion ever since.

> STEVE: Do you have any time to talk today?
>
> STEVE: I thought of you today when I was making guacamole. Why is yours so much better?
>
> STEVE: Isabelle was wondering if you'd be back in January at all? She wants to go shopping with you. She says you have the best style. And you know I can't help her! Ha.
>
> STEVE: Please. Call. When you can.

Rina gritted her teeth and thought long and hard about calling Steve. Just as always when they were apart, she missed him in every part of her body and soul and longed to have his arms around her. She could hear his voice in her head, asking her silly questions or talking about himself and his life. Since they'd met last spring, they'd kissed exactly eight times and cuddled several more. Once, they'd very nearly "gone all the way," which was a stupid phrase teenagers used that Rina had now begun to use in her own mind. But Steve was terrified of so much. Losing Laura had killed something in him.

Maybe Rina's mother's accident was a sign. Maybe it was proof Rina needed to stop dallying her life away out East.

Instead of calling, Rina texted.

> RINA: Tell Isabella I'll try to get out there before spring. I miss her.

> RINA: My father just wrote to say Mom's awake. It's the first time she's been conscious since the accident.

Steve wrote back right away.

> STEVE: Send them both my love.

Rina wanted to laugh. Her parents had no idea who Steve was. Since she'd met Steve, she'd hardly spoken to them at all. Once, she'd mentioned to them she was on Martha's Vineyard—but they'd assumed she was just on a case, and she hadn't corrected them. Since Martha's Vineyard had started out with a case, it hadn't felt like a lie.

Rina returned to her car and drove the rest of the way to the hospital, which was a two-story burnt-brown building that hunkered low to the ground. Out front, EMT workers took breaks by their ambulances, talking quietly as she strode past them and headed toward her mother's area of the hospital. Now that her mother had finally woken up, they'd moved her to a different ward.

Rina was surprised to find her father downstairs, buying a cup of coffee from a machine. He was ashen, and his gray hair was in wild clouds above both ears, but his eyes echoed relief. Since Rina's return on New Year's

Day, they'd hardly said more than a few words to one another. Now, he said, "Where did you go?"

Rina sensed the accusation behind the question. Despite the years of grievances and bad blood between them, it was still beyond her father's comprehension that she'd dared miss the exact moment her mother awoke.

"I had to go downtown for a few hours," Rina said.

"To do what?"

Rina swallowed the lump in her throat. Too distraught to do anything else, she'd popped in to see her childhood friend, Carmella, one of the only people in the world who understood the difficult dynamics between Rina and her parents. She'd wanted advice. Ultimately, Carmella had offered a shoulder to cry on as she'd muttered, "Your parents are difficult, Rina. They've always been that way."

"It was for a job," Rina lied.

Her father's face was stony. "Who went missing?"

"I'm not going to take the job."

Her father took a step toward her, nearly spilling his coffee from the Styrofoam cup. "Your mother would want you to find whoever it is."

"They've already been found," Rina said, raising her chin. "Let's go see Mom. Okay?"

* * *

Rina's parents, Wally and Ellen, had met as teenagers at Santa Monica High School and married shortly after graduation. Theirs was a story of love and joy that shouldn't have allowed a missing teenage girl. When Penny hadn't made it home that long-ago afternoon, Wally and Ellen had a decision to make. They could either blame one another or come together stronger than before. Ultimately, they'd decided on the latter. This incredible bond that had resulted hadn't allowed for anyone else. They'd left Rina in the metaphorical cold. In many ways, they'd stopped thinking about themselves as parents the moment Penny didn't come home.

But this lack of care for Rina had allowed Rina incredible freedom. She'd used that freedom to look for Penny—a herculean task that hadn't resulted in anything more than a few useless clues. But throughout this search, Rina had learned more about herself and the world than she'd ever known possible. And she'd cultivated skills she'd later used as a private investigator. It dramatically altered the course of her life.

Now, so many years after Penny didn't come home from school that day, Rina walked into the hospital room to find her mother, Ellen, half asleep in a hospital bed. Light shimmered in from the open window, and the seventy-five-degree temperature made it difficult for Rina to remember that just last week, she'd been up to her knees in snow on Martha's Vineyard.

Ellen was in her mid-sixties with soft blonde hair to her shoulders and bones that seemed a little too big for her body. Because of the accident, she was covered in bruises—across her cheek and along her arms and legs. She'd broken her left arm and her right ankle, and bandages were wrapped around her head.

When Rina had arrived in California on New Year's Day, she'd learned the accident hadn't been automobile-related. But when Rina had asked what kind of accident it had been, her father hadn't told her. This was another mystery Rina was left to solve.

Ellen's eyes fluttered open, and she turned her gaze

toward Rina. She seemed to size her up, demanding more of her than a newly conscious woman should have been able to.

But something about her mother was so broken. Rina's heart ached just seeing her like this.

"Mom?" Rina stepped toward the side of the bed and reached for her hand. "Mom, it's me. It's Rina."

Immediately, her mother's eyes grew shadowed. Rina turned to look at her father, whose eyes remained downcast.

"Where am I?" Ellen asked wistfully. "What is all this, Wally?"

Wally stepped around to the opposite side of the bed and took Ellen's other hand. "You were in an accident, honey," he explained. "And this is your daughter, Rina. You remember?"

Ellen's eyes flickered back toward Rina to size her up. She scowled. "I know who she is. I know what she did to our Penny."

Rina hurried away from the bed and smacked her back on the wall. Penny's name rang through the air between them. Before Rina could come up with something to say, something to calm her mother down, a nurse arrived to take Ellen's vitals, and Rina leaped out of the room and stumbled down the hall.

"Rina! Wait a second."

Rina stopped, touched the wall, and gasped for breath. Her mother hadn't brought up Penny in decades. Why now?

"She's not completely in her right mind," her father explained from behind her. "The doctors are calling it a form of amnesia caused by the accident."

Rina turned and blinked back tears.

"I didn't know she would bring that up," her father insisted. "And I'm sure she didn't mean it."

"We both know she did," Rina breathed.

"Rina, she's sick," Wally blared. "She needs you more than ever right now. And she needs your forgiveness."

But Rina was falling apart. Her mother's horrific face filled her mind's eye. "I just need some air," she said, stumbling toward the elevator.

"Come back up when you're ready," Wally begged. "We'll be here."

Rina rocketed back down to the ground floor and stomped through the halls, her heart pumping with anger and sorrow. Everywhere she looked, people nursed themselves back to health; they were bandaged and bruised; they wore eyepatches and stumbled along with walkers. Life seemed inescapable and tremendously cruel. Was pain really always the result?

Before Rina knew what she'd done, she pulled up Steve's number on her phone and listened as it blared across the continent. She could feel it ringing over Kansas fields, through the streets of Chicago, along Pennsylvanian highways, all the way to Steve in his mechanic's shop.

"Rina. Are you okay?" Steve sounded choked up.

Rina tugged her hair and blinked out across the parking lot. Her throat felt thick with tears. "I don't know," she answered finally. "I really don't."

Steve sighed into the phone. "Something has happened."

"What?" Rina couldn't make sense of what he said. "What do you mean?"

"I just got off the phone with Claire," Steve said.

"Gail is gone. She's missing. Nobody knows where she is."

And just like that, Rina found herself catapulted into yet another mystery. But she was beginning to think she couldn't handle any more of them. She could only take so much.

"What do you need me to do?"

"Everyone is pretty sure she'll show up," Steve stuttered, perhaps sensing the reticence in Rina's voice.

Rina breathed heavily through the receiver. She was on the verge of bursting into tears. Her mother's voice rang in her head: *I know what she did to our Penny.*

"Do they usually?" Steve asked.

"Do they usually what?"

"Do teenage girls like this usually show back up?"

Rina reached her car and placed her forehead on the edge, blinking through the tinted windows to see her sunglasses case, several take-out napkins, and a pair of earrings she'd removed that morning, deciding they weren't right for the hospital. Everything felt outside of time.

"Rina? Are you there?"

"I'm here," Rina rasped. "Teenage girls? You asked if they usually come home?"

"Yes. Rina, are you all right?"

"They usually come home," Rina said, rubbing her left eye so hard that she saw bright flashes of light. "They usually want to prove something. But that's not every case. That's not every girl."

Steve was quiet. Rina could picture him at the auto shop, his nose smeared with black from the bottom of somebody's car. That was how she'd initially met him, she remembered now. Her rental car kept turning off. She'd been in a crazy mood, on the verge of kicking the wheels until her toes were bruised. But Steve had stepped in and fixed it. He'd smiled at the volatility that surged from her —as though he accepted it, even when he didn't understand it.

"Keep me updated," Rina offered.

"Rina..." Steve whispered her name and Rina's heart felt squeezed. "Rina, maybe we should talk."

But Rina didn't have the energy for a conversation about "them," about "expectations," about the messy "will-they, won't-they" of the previous year. Her mother had just torn open old wounds and left her to bleed, metaphorically speaking, across the linoleum of the hospital floor.

"I have to go," Rina said. "Talk soon."

And she hung up.

Chapter Five

Claire and Russel sat in the waiting room outside the University of Massachusett's counseling office. Hardly noticing it, Claire shredded a pamphlet she'd picked up on the side table, one about "how to help your college-aged student from home." Pieces of paper fell to the ground.

Gail's counselor opened the door and greeted Claire and Russel by name. Claire leaped up and followed him into his office. It was decorated like something out of a university catalog, with a long mahogany desk, oil paintings of the river and trees near campus, and thick wooden bookshelves filled with novels and academic texts. Seth Alton, the counselor, was in his mid-thirties and balding, the last of his reddish hair clinging to his scalp.

Once upon a time, Russel had been balding, too. But he'd had implants. His head was bushy and thick, the sort of thing Claire had once loved to swirl her fingers through.

"Please, sit down." Seth gestured toward the chairs in front of his desk.

Claire and Russel sat, Claire at the very front of the chair, like a nervous student in class. "Thank you for meeting with us so quickly."

Seth glanced at the box of tissue on the desk. It looked as though he'd put it there just for Claire and Russel. As though he'd expected this meeting to be messy.

"Clear this up for me," Seth began. "You haven't heard from your daughter in how long?"

"She didn't come back to the dorm two days ago," Claire said.

"It was less than forty-eight hours ago," Russel said. "She left that afternoon and never came home that night."

"Is it possible she's just crashing with a friend this week?" Seth asked. "The first week back after Christmas break is always a bit foggy for the students. They party a little too hard because they don't have as many academic responsibilities and forget themselves. Just walking across campus this morning, I saw what looked to be five zombies carrying bottles of vodka."

"She lives with her twin sister," Claire blared, interrupting him, hating how angry she sounded. "And Abby hasn't heard from Gail, either."

"Did they get into an argument of some kind?" Seth asked.

"Yes," Russel bucked in. "They weren't speaking very much over Christmas break."

Seth gave Russel a half smile as though that cleared things up considerably. "To me, that means Gail is off somewhere with a friend, cooling off. Maybe she wants to apply to change rooms. That happens here all the time. We could even bring someone else into Abby's room.

Someone who isn't happy with their current circumstances."

"You don't understand," Claire said. "This isn't normal behavior. My twins were thick as thieves until last week. Something happened."

Seth raised his shoulders, and he looked like a teenager pretending to be an adult. "There's not a lot we can do right now. We can talk to some of Gail's classmates and friends. But if you're saying Abby is her closest friend, doesn't it stand to reason that Abby probably knows where she is? Maybe she's just not telling you?"

Claire sizzled with anger. This man was suggesting that both of her daughters were lying to her. It wasn't possible.

"Abby wants to come home with us until Gail is found," Claire said. "The woman on the phone said we could talk to you about that. About switching her to online classes."

Seth leaned back in his chair and rubbed his temples. He was beginning to lose interest. "Sure. But please translate to your daughter the importance of being in class as soon as possible. We see so many students slip away when they go online."

Claire wanted to scream again. This man was worried about Abby's academic failings during the second semester of her freshman year (a year that arguably hardly mattered in the grand scheme of things) while her other daughter was out there somewhere, missing.

It was impossible to translate how close Gail and Abby had always been. Seth hadn't been there when they'd taken their first steps together, holding hands.

Claire and Russel walked across campus toward

Abby's dorm room. An icy wind swept between them, tossing Russel's hair. He'd recently dyed away his grays, and he looked about ten years younger. From his recent stints at the gym, his shoulders were broader than ever. He looked as though he could throw Claire over his shoulder and swagger across the rolling hills of campus through the limestone buildings from centuries ago.

Claire strung her arm through Russel's and pressed her cheek against his bicep. She shook with sorrow.

"I don't know what to do with myself," she whispered. "I've always known where my girls were. I've always been the kind of mother they tell things to."

"She'll turn up, Claire," Russel said. "She's eighteen and acting out. As soon as she senses we're giving her the attention she craves, she'll come back to us."

Claire furrowed her brow. "You really think it's that simple?"

"Our girls are still growing and changing," Russel went on. "They're experimenting with adulthood. They're figuring out who they are."

When they reached the dorm room, Abby tore open the door and threw herself in Claire's arms. Her face was blotchy, and she hadn't showered that day or, it seemed, the day before. Russel stood in the shadows of the dorm, his eyes tracing the twin beds and the messy desks. There was a photograph of the four of them on Abby's desk, taken on a family vacation from last summer. They'd gone to Florida. Abby had suffered a terrible sunburn, and Gail had nursed her back to health, smearing aloe vera across her shoulders.

Claire would have given anything to go back to that day. Everything had felt so clear.

"Mom, I don't know what to do. I can't eat. I can't sleep." Abby tugged at her red hair and paced in front of her messy bed.

Claire's stomach twisted. The number one thing she wanted to do, she realized, was go through Gail's things before they left. She wanted to look for clues. She eyed Gail's desk and drawers curiously.

"Why don't you and your dad go grab something to eat?" Claire suggested.

Abby's chin trembled.

"That sounds great, honey," Russel offered. "What was that restaurant you took me to last time? It was delicious."

"Ralph's," Abby said, her voice quivering.

"I'll pack up your things," Claire promised. "And we'll be on the road in no time."

Russel and Abby stepped into the hallway and closed the door behind them. This left Claire in the echoing mess of her daughters' dorm room. Because so many generations of students had lived here, a consistent rank smell existed beneath everything, as though mold grew between the stones of the walls.

Claire had once read an article about mold spores. About how they were dangerous for your mind if you breathed in too many. People had entered psychoses. People had gone mad. Had that happened to Gail?

Claire set to work on Gail's desk. She was delicate, leafing through pieces of paper and notebooks, looking for clues. She found Gail's student card and a debit card that had just expired a few months ago. (Claire had, of course, been the one to order the new card.) There were notes from the classes Gail had taken last semester, second-hand books that looked like they'd gone through a shredder, and numerous chapsticks and lipsticks that looked to have cost two dollars at most.

Frustrated, Claire dug through Gail's bed and looked underneath. It occurred to her that Gail's laptop was nowhere to be found; neither was her phone. When she searched through her drawers, she realized that pieces of clothing were also missing. Sweatshirts. A dress they'd bought together on their trip to Florida. Numerous pairs of underwear and bras. And her backpack and small suitcase were gone, too.

She'd intended to go. She'd planned it. She'd packed.

Claire sat at the edge of Gail's bed and then collapsed back into the sheets, inhaling Gail's scent. She remembered how she'd looked two days before as Claire had driven her back: forlorn, angry, her eyes bloodshot and lined with black. What had Claire missed?

Last summer at a family barbecue, Claire had asked Rina about her work as a private investigator. And Rina had said something about getting into the heads of the missing people. "I try to imagine I am them. What did they see before they disappeared? What could have led them down this path? What kind of people did they hang out with?"

"It's like writing fiction," Kelli had suggested. "You have to make up a character in your head."

"Something like that," Rina said. "Although I have to admit, this is much easier with people I don't know. When I do know them, even a little bit, my perception of them clouds my judgment."

Claire had thought this was fascinating—that those you loved and knew the most were the most difficult to find. Perhaps it was because they knew how to hide from you the most.

Claire packed Abby's bags, locked the dorm room, and met Abby and Russel at Ralph's. They'd ordered her a BLT and french fries, but Claire wasn't hungry at all. She felt weight drifting off her middle, her thighs. They boxed up the food, paid the bill, and headed out to the family van, which would feel lopsided without Gail.

"Abby, honey?" Claire began from the front seat, rubbing lotion into her chapped hands. "Did you ask any of your friends where she might have gone? Is there anyone else we should call?"

"Nobody's heard from her," Abby said.

Claire turned to look her daughter in the eye. After the counselor said Abby probably knew more than she was letting on, Claire wanted to hunt for clues in her face. But there was nothing. Only grief.

"She packed a bag," Claire said. "She took her laptop and her clothes. It feels like she had a plan."

Abby raised her shoulders as tears shimmered down her cheeks. She didn't know.

Claire turned back around and watched the road for a while. It was early January, which meant the gold-plated beauty of the Christmas season had given way to grim grays and dead grass. Wind crashed against the minivan, making it shiver on the road. Russel had always been an excellent driver, focused and sure of himself. Even now, he had his hands at ten and two.

Think, Claire. Come on. Imagine you're Rina. Imagine you're tracking someone down.

All at once, Claire remembered the expired debit card in Gail's things. Didn't that mean that Gail had her other debit card on her? The one Claire had given her? Because all of the girls' food had already been paid for via the campus service, the girls' cards were technically only for emergencies and the occasional fun night out. Claire and Russel had first given them out when the girls were sixteen. They'd been very responsible about money, sticking to Claire's stipulations.

But if Gail was out there somewhere, she'd had to have used her card. Maybe that would help Claire track her down.

Claire pulled up the family bank account, her heart pounding. Gail and Abby each had a separate account that was linked to Claire and Russel's, which meant she could see everything.

But when Claire pulled up the account, all the blood drained from her cheeks.

Two days ago, Gail had emptied the account— all three hundred dollars. She'd done it at an ATM right on campus. It was a dead end.

"What's up?" Russel had noticed Claire's fresh panic.

Claire shoved her phone back in her purse and returned her gaze to the foggy horizon.

"Claire? What's going on?" Russel demanded.

"She emptied her bank account." Claire's voice was quiet.

"There couldn't have been that much in it."

"Three hundred."

"That won't get her very far," Russel went on. "She'll come running back."

Claire's heart pounded. A part of her considered putting more money into the account, just so Gail had cash wherever she was. Just so she could eat. Just so she could find a warm place to sleep. But maybe Russel was right. Maybe it was best to hold out and wait for her to figure out how weak she was when faced with a cruel and cold world.

Chapter Six

Rina couldn't sleep. As dawn crept across the West Coast, casting them in golds and pinks, Rina donned running shorts, a sports bra, and her tennis shoes and walked outside. As she ran, she stretched her legs out as long as she could, and her bob flashed across her ears. Not long after she'd begun, more joggers descended upon the boardwalk. Some of them conducted business meetings on their earpieces, barking orders at someone on the East Coast. Annoyance made Rina stagger to a halt. She wandered away from the runners and onto the sand, where she removed her shoes and gazed out across the frothing waves.

Not long after she sat, she realized this wasn't any old beach. She'd almost been arrested here nearly thirty years ago. She hadn't thought about it in years.

She'd been seventeen at the time. Penny had been gone for a little more than a year. The abyss that had opened up with Penny's disappearance had nearly swallowed Rina whole. She clung to whatever she could of the real world as a way to remind herself she remained alive.

That summer, she'd clung hardest to her boyfriend Cody, who never pushed her to talk of Penny. They drank beers and wine coolers; they drove too fast down the highway; their kisses were filled with yearning. Rina could almost pretend she was a normal teenager.

On that night when Rina was seventeen, her mother and father had just left again. Ellen had written a note that said they'd be back next week without any mention of where they were off to. This was typical behavior by then. After Penny's disappearance, it was as though being at home with Rina reminded them too much of what they'd lost. They hardly spoke to her; they didn't go to any of her high school theater productions or her tennis matches. It was as though, with the loss of their younger daughter, they'd decided to throw the first one away, too.

That night, there was a party at Carmella's place. Carmella's parents were visiting her aunt in Malibu, and Carmella wanted to have a few people over to swim in the pool and drink beers. As things did in Santa Monica, it quickly got out of control. By the time Cody and Rina arrived, they had a healthy buzz from drinking on the beach, and Carmella was more than tipsy, diving into the pool and rising up to do Jell-O shots in greens, purples and reds. Music pumped from the stereo.

Rina changed into her swimsuit and swam alongside Carmella. Her long brunette hair spiraled through the chlorinated water. Cody jumped into the pool, splashing water across the teenagers who tanned across the beach chairs. They screeched, and Rina went under the water to giggle to herself. She and Cody reached out for one another and kissed underwater, pretending they were in a movie scene. Being teenagers in such a ridiculously beautiful location, where parents made more money than they often knew what to do with only blocks away from horrendous homelessness, meant being forever cynical about the way the world worked.

Rina and Cody climbed out of the pool to eat burgers and chips and grab another round of beers. As they passed the grill, Rina froze at the sound of Penny's name. Immediately, the crowd quieted. Rina glared at them, considering throwing her fresh beer over one of their heads. She knew how much Santa Monica liked to gossip about Penny and what had happened to her. It was fodder for them. Just another thing to talk about at pool parties. She hated it.

"Don't give them the satisfaction," Cody urged, tugging her along.

Sometime after nightfall, Jimmy, a friend of Cody's, arrived with a trunkful of fireworks. Jimmy suggested they head out to the beach and set off fireworks. Rina could do nothing but run after him, screaming at the top of her lungs.

Rina, Cody, Jimmy, and a few others giggled on the dark beach and set up the first firework. Jimmy explained his cousin had purchased them illegally in Utah and driven them across the border. This made the entire operation feel even more exciting. More alive.

As the first fireworks tore through the night sky, hissing and popping into neon colors, Rina leaned her head against Cody's chest and tried to imagine that wherever she was, Penny could see the fireworks, too. Maybe she would understand the fireworks were a signal from her sister, who still loved her. "I'm going to find you, Penny," Rina breathed to the black sky. "Mark my words."

Just then, sirens joined the sound of fireworks. Cop cars pulled up across the beach. The teenagers scattered, drunkenly running through the night, their feet ripping through the sand. But Rina and Cody were too intoxicated to make it far. Three cops cornered them, their hands waving. They shone flashlights in their faces.

Through the chaos, Rina started laughing. She couldn't help it. When compared to the loneliness she felt at home and the ache in her heart, this all felt tremendously funny. She burrowed her face in Cody's chest, trying to stop, but she couldn't. Too drunk to care, Cody laughed, too. They looked like fools.

"Wait a minute," one of the cops said. "Is that you, Rina?"

Rina quieted at the sound of her name. She turned on her heel and blinked through the night at one of the cops who'd been charged to search for her sister. He'd interviewed her numerous times, hunting through her words for some comprehension. But she hadn't known anything.

"Do you need a ride home?" the officer asked.

It was suddenly clear that she wouldn't get in trouble. That this officer would help her.

It was all because he felt bad for her. More than that, he and everyone else in Santa Monica knew that Rina's parents had all but abandoned her since Penny's disappearance. Everyone pitied her.

"You should arrest me," Rina said. "I broke the law."

But the cop wasn't having it. Even more pity filled his eyes. Everyone on the beach understood the truth—Rina wanted to be arrested if only to get her parents' attention. To remind them she was still there. That she still needed them.

* * *

Rina walked along the beach where she'd once set off fireworks with Cody and Jimmy. She could still feel the fireworks ringing in her ears and the euphoria as she'd rushed head-long across the sand, away from the cops. She'd felt like Thelma or Louise, wild and free.

Rina went home to shower and returned to the hospital for a meeting with her mother's doctor. The physician was a forty-something man with a California tan and teeth a little too bright for the orange tint of his face. An online search had told Rina that Dr. Bartlett was one of the best in the hospital. A more furtive search via Rina's friend in the private detective world hadn't found anything amiss on Dr. Bartlett's file, so she had to trust him.

Dr. Bartlett showed Rina the x-rays they'd taken, along with photographs of her significant bruises.

"Despite all this, we think she'll make a full recovery by spring," he went on. "She's healing up quickly. She might need some light physical therapy, but nothing major."

Rina felt a swell of relief. "My father won't tell me how the accident happened? When I first got out here, I assumed it was automobile-related, but..."

The doctor shook his head. "Your father is telling us she fell on the boardwalk. But her bruises and breaks suggest something much more drastic. That's part of the reason I wanted to meet with you today." He paused and wet his lips. "Does your father have a history of violence?"

Rina's heart pounded. "No. I mean, not that I've ever seen. They've been together since they were teenagers. To be honest with you, they've always liked each other much more than they like me."

Dr. Bartlett gave no indication he'd heard her joke. "As you've probably noticed, your mother has suffered a form of traumatic amnesia. This can happen after a fall of this magnitude."

"Right." Rina thought again of her mother's cruelty. To Rina, that had always been bubbling at the surface, ready to attack.

"We hope her memory will return to her soon," Dr. Bartlett continued. "Maybe then, she'll be able to explain what happened to her. In the event that your father did have something to do with it, we will be obligated to contact the authorities."

"I just can't imagine that," Rina said. "And trust me. I'm not the biggest fan of my father."

Dr. Bartlett raised his shoulders. "You'd be surprised what we see here at the hospital. There is no telling what people are capable of."

Chapter Seven

With Abby back home, Claire struggled to let her out of her sight. When she sequestered herself in her bedroom, presumably to do homework, attend an online class, or chat with friends, Claire paced downstairs, scrubbed the kitchen counters, or pretended to read quietly, constantly listening for the sound of Abby on the staircase. When she heard it, she popped up and hurried to invite Abby for a snack or an hour of television. Anything to keep her close. Her biggest fear was that Abby would somehow go down the staircase, slip out the front door, and disappear to wherever it was Gail hid.

The day after Abby's return, Russel had a business meeting in the city. Claire helped him pack, hanging his suits in a carrier and bustling around the bedroom to line the suitcase with clean socks.

"I'm sure they'd understand if you told them you couldn't make it," Claire said, pausing over the suitcase and wringing her hands. "Your daughter is missing for crying out loud."

Russel was still in his boxers and an undershirt. He looked tremendously handsome, like an advertisement model for an underwear campaign, and he ruffled his dyed hair and sighed. "You know how important this is to me, Claire."

Not so very long ago, Russel had worked for the city council at Oak Bluffs. However, after a significant amount of funds had been stolen from the city council, the city decided to blame Russel. This had been hugely traumatic for Russel, a man who loved Oak Bluffs with his heart and soul and had been willing to do anything for his community. Although Susan had been instrumental in proving Russel wasn't the one to blame (it had actually been Kelli's ex-husband, Mike), Russel had felt blindsided and let down by his community. He'd quit not long afterward and gotten a job in property development, which frequently took him into New York. "I always dreamed of something bigger than working for the city council," he'd told Claire. "Now, I realize that all the work I did for Oak Bluffs feeds directly into my work for the city."

And if Claire was honest with herself, she often liked it when Russel went away. He was a domineering force in her life, the sort of man who wanted things to be just so. More often than not, he suggested she change something about her appearance, her cooking, or the house; he rarely complimented all the work she did. And he often ridiculed the flower shop, asking why people cared about buying flowers in this day and age, anyway. When she got upset, Russel said he was just teasing her. "Why can't I joke with you anymore?" he'd said.

It wasn't clear to Claire when this tension had begun. In her memory, Russel was the tender city councilman she'd fallen in love with years and years ago. He was sturdy and funny and a loving father. Only when he returned from his trips to the city did she realize this version of Russel wasn't the version she'd fallen in love with.

But then again, people changed. People grew. And being married didn't mean you weren't allowed too anymore. In fact, changing and growing alongside one another was a part of being married. Maybe Claire just hadn't gotten the memo on how to change yet.

The morning after Russel left, Abby padded downstairs in a pair of sweatpants and a big sweatshirt and poured herself a cup of coffee. Her cheeks were hollow, and her eyes were red. "Rachel is doing online classes, too," she said. "She couldn't stand being on campus, trying to pretend everything was all right."

"Oh, honey." Claire touched her heart. "Is she going to Orcas Island to be with Aunt Charlotte?"

Just then, Claire's phone buzzed on the countertop. It was Charlotte.

"We were just talking about you."

Charlotte's voice sounded strained, as though she, too, had been crying. "Rachel and I are on the ferry."

Claire leaned against the countertop as her stomach thudded with dread. Charlotte coming like this meant that Gail's disappearance was real. It was actually happening and affecting people outside their immediate family.

Although it had felt like an eternity, it had only been four days since Gail left. Claire had parroted to Charlotte what Russel had said, that Gail was probably just off somewhere, biding her time, trying to get attention. Charlotte hadn't believed Claire for a second.

Charlotte and Rachel drove directly to Claire's house. Charlotte swallowed Claire in a hug as Rachel and Abby scampered toward the staircase, wanting to talk upstairs.

"Girls?" Claire stepped away from Charlotte and glared at them. "Can you do your talking down here, please?"

She couldn't stand that they had secrets from her. Was it possible they knew exactly what had happened? Was it possible they were just watching Claire's misery and not solving it?

"We brought food and wine," Charlotte said, gesturing toward the bags at her feet, filled with groceries.

"You didn't have to come back," Claire stuttered. "I know you have things to do out West. You have a life."

Charlotte squeezed Claire's elbow. "You're my life."

Claire, Abby, Rachel, and Charlotte carried the groceries to the kitchen. Charlotte sliced tomatoes, onions, and garlic; she wanted to make shakshuka. The clock on the stove said it was only ten thirty, but Claire cranked open a bottle of red and poured them two glasses. Abby and Rachel drank coffee and sat quietly on the couch with their laptops in front of them. They were officially "attending classes," but they'd put the video on mute.

Abstractly, Claire wondered if Abby would ever return to college. Maybe this would prove to be too distressing for her. Maybe all her hopes for the future would fade.

Charlotte served them shakshuka with fresh bread, and they ate it in the breakfast nook as January sunlight flitted between clouds like froth outside. It had been a long time since Claire had enjoyed breakfast—or any meal for that matter—and she allowed herself, briefly, to engage with the spices and tomato flavors. The fresh bread was invigorating; she tore it and scraped it through the sauce, closing her eyes against the nutty flavor.

After breakfast, Abby and Rachel washed the dishes. Charlotte poured herself a second glass of wine, and Claire nodded toward her own glass, ready to drift into another state of consciousness. It had been a long time since she'd drunk during the day with her sister. But she just wanted to fall away from herself for a little while.

"You told the counselor you still haven't heard from her?" Charlotte asked, swirling her wine through her glass.

"I talked to him this morning," Claire said. "He's just like Russel. He still thinks she'll turn up at a boyfriend's or a friend's. He thinks she's partying the days away."

"It just doesn't sound like Gail."

Claire shook her head. "Girls do change a lot at the age of eighteen," she stuttered. "They experiment. They look for boundaries."

"But they don't break their mothers' hearts without reason," Charlotte said. "If Gail really did run away like this, on purpose, something pushed her there. Something happened."

Abby and Rachel returned to the living room couch, where they set themselves up with their next online classes. Charlotte and Claire remained at the breakfast nook, talking intermittently and watching snow spit from the heavens. New Year's Eve now felt like months ago. Claire now understood why trauma-aged people.

"I tried to look for clues," Claire was saying. "But that's how I figured out she'd emptied her bank account. That scared me. I can't imagine how Rina does this work all the time. It's terrifying to stare into the abyss, wondering where she fell."

"Have you reached out to Rina?"

Claire shook her head.

"Why not?" Charlotte asked. "Even if Steve and Rina aren't, you know, 'together,' she's still a friend of the family. She would do everything she could to find Gail."

Claire raised her shoulders. "Rina handles real cases. Cases with criminals. Cases that deal with violence. I don't want to distract her with something like this."

Fear dripped from her words. Why hadn't she allowed herself to fully consider this side of things?

"I don't think we should rule anything out," Charlotte whispered. "Rina wouldn't tell us to, anyway."

Claire rubbed her temples and gazed across the yard's dead grass. Unlike most of her family members, she and Russel didn't have the capital to purchase a coastal home. This had been yet another contributing factor to Russel seeking a new job. He'd wanted to "set them up." He'd wanted a gorgeous, coastal home. He'd wanted to fish outside his door.

"Why don't we just call Steve and talk it over?" Charlotte suggested. "He's your older brother. He'd do anything for you."

Claire put the phone on speakerphone. She first dialed Steve's number, but it went to voicemail. After that, she called Steve's auto shop, and Isabella answered on the third ring.

"Montgomery Autos," she said. "How can I help you?"

"Hey, Bella," Claire said, her voice wavering.

"Aunt Claire!" Isabella sounded immediately stricken. "How are you? Have you found Gail?"

"No," Claire said. "We haven't."

Isabella was quiet.

"Can we talk to your dad?" Charlotte asked.

"Sure. He's in the shop. I'll grab him."

Steve was breathless when he answered, as though he'd burst from working beneath a truck and scrambled to the phone. "Claire. Charlotte. Are you all right?" He stuttered. "That's a ridiculous question right now. I know."

Claire locked eyes with Charlotte. All she wanted right now was for Charlotte to take the reins.

"We were wondering if Rina's still in town?" Charlotte began. "We'd love to pick her brain."

"Oh. Um, no. She's not." Steve sighed.

Claire remembered what Charlotte had said about Rina running out of the New Year's Eve party. It had looked like a breakup. Steve's tone half confirmed this.

"Would you mind reaching out to her for us?" Charlotte went on. "We wouldn't ask if it wasn't serious."

"Of course," Steve said. "I'll give her a call today. She has connections, you know. People in the industry who can dig into things."

"That's what we need," Charlotte affirmed.

"Claire?" Steve's voice was quieter. "Claire, I'm so sorry this is happening." He sounded choked up. "I'm going to do anything I can to find her, okay?"

"You and Rina broke up, didn't you?" Claire interjected.

Steve sighed deeply into the phone. "We were never anything. Not that I know of, anyway."

Claire and Charlotte eyed one another over the table. Charlotte's face echoed doubt.

"She'll answer my call if that's what you're worried about," Steve said. He sounded like the confident, proud older brother Claire had always admired. She had to trust him.

"I love you," Claire said. "Thank you."

"I love you both," Steve assured them. "We're going to find her."

Chapter Eight

Rina was at the hospital till late morning. She sat on a plastic chair by her mother's bedside, watching the sunlight play out across her worn face, which was smeared with bruises. Her father had gone to a doctor's appointment of his own, which was a merciful relief. Rina didn't want to look at him. She didn't want to consider the idea that he'd hurt her mother. It was too alienating.

Minutes before Rina planned to depart for the day, Steve called her. It was the fortieth time since yesterday. It had come with twelve text messages, all of which read: **"Please, call me back. I need to talk to you."** But Rina had been dealing with her own private demons. She couldn't deal with Steve's.

"What is that racket?" Ellen's eyes flipped open, and she glared at Rina and Rina's buzzing phone. "And what are you doing here? Aren't you off to Timbuktu? Or wherever it is, you make your money?"

Rina swallowed the lump in her throat. "How are you feeling, Mom?"

Ellen shifted and scrunched her face as though pain rocketed through her body when she moved. "Where's Wally? What did you do to him?"

Rina yearned to roll her eyes, but she didn't. Instead, she reached for the glass of water on the table and helped her mother drink from its straw. She had a flash of a memory of her mother doing that years ago—helping Rina drink juice when she'd had strep throat. It had been rare for her mother to do something so tender. Perhaps that was why it had stuck with her.

Rina left before her father arrived. She made her way down the staircase, too frightened to use the elevator, worried the doors would burst open to reveal Wally himself. The sunlight blistered her face in the parking lot, and she donned a large pair of Gucci sunglasses. Just then, she would have given anything to be working a case somewhere else in the world, digging through someone else's secrets rather than her own family's.

What did she know? That her mother was injured and didn't remember what happened. That her father wasn't telling the whole story. And that, many years ago, her sister had disappeared—and they still had no idea what had happened. It was a terrible story. And she couldn't make sense of it.

Rina left her car at the hospital and wandered barefoot along the beach for a while. Again, Steve called, but she ignored it. As a gust of Pacific wind rushed across her face, something tugged at her mind, something she'd forgotten. Suddenly, she remembered what Steve had said during their last phone conversation. His niece was missing. Since then, she'd told herself that people in the Montgomery family didn't just go missing, and they didn't need her help. As she'd fallen through memories in Santa Monica, she'd let the news trickle out of her mind.

That wasn't like her. But she wasn't sure she recognized herself right now.

Rina told herself she'd call Steve back later tonight and kept walking past the Ferris wheel and around the mini market where she, Penny, and Cody had eaten ice cream cones and drunk soda. Very soon, she turned the corner and approached Santa Monica High School, a sturdy red brick building with three stories, a football field with AstroTurf, immaculate tennis courts, and a billboard out front that said: "The Santa Monica Fighting Trojans!"

Rina hadn't been back to her high school since graduation. She could still remember how it smelled: like gym clothes, bubble gum, and cheap cologne. Like thousands of pubescent teens, all with private hopes, dreams, and body odors. As she got closer and closer, she imagined Cody stepping out from the front door in his letterman jacket and nodding hello. She imagined them kissing against the tennis shed as the wind fluttered through her hair.

Although it was technically trespassing, Rina stepped onto the property and strode past the front door. It was just past twelve-thirty, which meant the kids were in lunch, eating slices of pizza that tasted vaguely of cardboard and drinking cartons of milk. She imagined the small dramas at lunch tables—the breakups, the teasing.

Half expecting someone to barge out and tell Rina she shouldn't be there, Rina hurried around the corner and toward the back of the high school. She didn't dare hope it was still there, but when she saw it, she nearly fell to her knees.

After Penny had disappeared and it became clear she wasn't coming back, Santa Monica High School had had a fundraiser to make a mural for Penny. It was five feet high and ten feet across. Jefferson Hutchins, the best painter at the high school at the time, had painted Penny as she'd been back then, smiling out from the exterior wall thoughtfully. She was writing in her journal, her pen poised. Rina knew the image well. She'd taken the photograph they'd used for the painting.

Funnily enough, it looked as though there had been recent touch-ups on the painting. Rina imagined a current high schooler carefully fixing what the weather had done to the image. This was so many years after Rina had last seen Penny's face.

Now that Rina saw the image again, she was transported back to that long-ago day when she'd taken the photograph. It was maybe six months before Penny had disappeared. Rina was sixteen, and Penny was fifteen or close to it. They were on the back porch of the home where her parents still lived, writing or drawing and listening to music on their boombox. Rina could practically hear the mid-90s hip hop and grunge. Mariah Carey. Madonna. Michael and Janet Jackson. They'd jumped up frequently to dance, swaying their hips.

That had been the night they'd had the boys over. Cody had come, as had Penny's crush and all of their other friends. They'd played music as loud as the boombox could go. The boys had brought beers, and Rina had been anxious, watching her sister to make sure she didn't drink too many.

Where had their parents been?

Rina leaned against the wall, racking her mind for more memories. This had been the one and only party they'd ever had at their parents' place. Perhaps they would have had more if Penny hadn't gone away.

Suddenly, the memory smacked her over the head.

Their parents had been gone. They'd left for vacation —without Penny and Rina—telling them that they needed alone time. They needed space.

Rina remembered laughing with Penny about this.

"It's like they didn't know what it would be like to have children," Penny said. "They did not think things through before they had us."

"I'm surprised they even had a second kid," Rina teased. "Once they realized how hard it was with me, why did they keep going?"

Penny swatted Rina on the calf and reached for a Twizzler, which she ate languidly, her eyes closed against the sharp sunlight.

"Maybe one day they'll fake their deaths and abandon us," Penny said.

Rina laughed. "They'll have different identities. New passports."

"They'll move to Paris or Bangkok or Buenos Aires," Penny went on. "And when people ask them why they don't have children, they'll say, 'Children hold you back from what you really want in life!' And they'll laugh like villains in the movies."

Rina cackled. She could imagine her mother in a fur coat somewhere, her lips bright red, her cheekbones sharper than ever. She could imagine her father buying an expensive luxury car, which he so often complained he couldn't afford because of "family responsibilities."

"What will we do when they go away?" Rina asked.

"We'll pretend they're not," Penny went on. "We can't have the authorities separating us. They hardly come to our school stuff, anyway. It's not like anyone would notice."

Now, as Rina leaned against the mural of her sister so many years after that day, she placed her hand over her sister's cheek. It was hard concrete and so unlike the real thing. Rina's eyes filled with tears. She'd forgotten, she realized now, that her parents had never wanted to be their parents. She'd forgotten that their dismissal of Rina had begun long before Penny had gone.

"I'm sorry I never found you," Rina whispered up to Penny's mural.

It was true that she'd looked. She'd gotten a substantial scholarship to the University of California, Berkeley, which was a sizable distance from her parents' place in Santa Monica. From there, she hadn't needed to contact her parents at all—not for money or emotional support. With Cody away in Europe, she'd felt completely alone for the first time in her life and thrown herself into her search for her sister.

But back then, she didn't have the proper tools and didn't know the right people to guide her. She'd gone over the police report, interviewed the officers who'd studied Penny's case, and spoke with Penny's boyfriend at the time, hunting for clues, but she got nowhere.

A few times over the years, Rina had dug into it again, searching, wondering. But by now, Penny's case was ice cold. With each person she found, each case she figured out, she still felt haunted by this first one and all she'd lost.

Rina returned to the hospital to fetch her car, then drove back home. It was midafternoon, but she was exhausted and dreaming of tucking herself in bed and sleeping the day away.

When she turned down her street, she spotted a dark blue vehicle in her driveway. Being a private investigator had cursed her because her first thought was something sinister. In truth, it was probably just someone lost, someone who'd pulled over to look at their phone.

Rina couldn't get into the driveway because whoever it was had parked in the very center. Muttering angrily to herself, she parked on the street (which would cost her) and hurried up toward the vehicle. It had a rental sticker on it. It was someone far from home.

"Hey," Rina began as she headed toward the driver's side. "Can I help you?"

Rina stopped short and gaped at the man in the front seat. It was Steve. He'd brought his seat back and pulled his hat over his eyes, and he was fast asleep, his lips partially opened. Even now, peering at him through the tinted windows of the rental, Rina's heart thudded with a mix of intrigue and adoration. He'd come all the way out West to see her. He wasn't willing to let whatever this was between them die.

All those phone calls had meant he was on his way. He needed her.

And he'd come right when she needed him the most.

Chapter Nine

The day after Charlotte and Rachel returned to Martha's Vineyard, the four of them had set off for the library to print photographs of Gail. On the pamphlets, they decided to list simple information:

MISSING: eighteen years old, red hair and green eyes, born islander, last seen on the campus of the University of Massachusetts. Contact the Montgomery's for details and any info you might have.

They printed five hundred copies and split into teams: Abby with Claire and Rachel with Charlotte.

The girls had wanted to go alone, but Claire was jumpy. She worried they'd go off somewhere and never be heard from again.

Claire and Abby roamed downtown, putting pamphlets up at coffee shops, restaurants, bars, telephone polls, and at the office near the ferry docks, where guests waited for their boats. For over two hours, they walked without speaking, taping and stapling. Claire wondered if they'd ever find something to say to one another again or have a casual conversation. Passersby said hello with sorrowful eyes, knowing the other twin was missing. Many of them said, "I'll keep an eye out for her," or "We're praying for you." But they felt like hollow words.

Claire beckoned for Abby to follow her inside when they neared the flower shop. She hadn't been there since the day before she'd driven the girls back to college, and the CLOSED sign on the door was ominous. It looked as though it had been abandoned a long time ago. When they entered, the smell of dying flowers was rank and powerful, like a funeral home times ten, and Abby coughed several times. Claire kept the front door open and hurried around to yank open windows to let the smell out. She probably lost upward of a thousand dollars in inventory, maybe more. But she couldn't dwell on that right now.

Claire fetched trash bags from a low drawer and passed a few to Abby. "Can you start shoving flowers in here?" She wanted to scrub the floors and the windows. She wanted something to be under control, for once.

Abby did as she was told, quietly dropping bouquets into trash bags and roaming through the shop. Claire got on her business computer, where she read emails from unhappy customers who'd come to the shop to pick up their bouquets only to find it closed. The emails filtered off after a few days, presumably because word had gotten around that Gail was gone. They knew not to bother Claire anymore.

Claire watched Abby roam wordlessly through the flower shop. Abby's hair was perpetually unwashed these days and tangled, wrapping into itself like a knotted sailing rope. Claire didn't look much better, she knew. Still, this version of Abby was such a contrast to the Abby she'd once known. Not so long ago, she and Gail had run around the flower shop, pretending to be fairies or princesses, tending to the bouquets or watering the plants. They'd adored Claire's "magical kingdom of flowers." And Claire had been happy to show them that you could make a living with such a beautiful, traditional trade.

Now, Russel was chasing cash in the city, and Gail was gone.

Abby's sniffling brought Claire from her reverie.

"Honey?" Claire jumped around the front desk and hurried toward her daughter, who was curled over the trash bag and heaving with tears. Claire wrapped her arms around her, and Abby shook, unable to speak.

"I know," Claire breathed. "It's so hard. It's terrible."

Abby rubbed her eyes and straightened her posture. She looked as though she'd just woken up.

"You don't have to keep doing this. I'll clean it up later," Claire assured her. The flowers were the least of her worries. "I'm sorry I asked you to."

"That's not it." Abby turned to look at her mother. In her face, Claire saw so many of her family members—her mother's kind eyes, Charlotte's thick but sculpted eyebrows, Kelli's strong cheekbones. "I just haven't been totally truthful with you. And I don't know how to say it."

Claire felt as though she was falling. It took everything within her to stay upright and be a guiding light to her daughter. But she wanted to scream.

"What is it, honey?"

Abby swallowed and stared at the ground. "Something happened on New Year's Eve."

Claire remembered the party through a series of sepia images. She remembered Uncle Wes on one knee, preparing to propose. She remembered Charlotte dancing with Everett. She remembered hugs and kisses, popped champagne, salmon puffs, music, and an entire inn brimming with laughter.

And, of course, Gail was in her mind's eye, moody, stomping through the party as though she had a vendetta against the entire family. Abby and Rachel had scampered after her, their faces marred with confusion and shock. Claire had brushed it off at the time, calling it a teenager's impulse. A teenager's mood.

"A few hours before the party, Gail came into my room and said she needed to tell me something," Abby began. "She was really pale, and she looked like she'd been crying. I was really busy with something. Like, this is totally not important, but I was texting this guy from school. Someone I have a big crush on. Or had a big crush on before the world ended." Abby sniffed. "Anyway, Gail started blabbing about something I didn't understand. She was basically sobbing. I kept asking her to repeat herself. And finally, I got the gist of what she was saying.

"Basically, she was talking about Dad. About how he wasn't who we thought he was. About how he wants to leave us and doesn't care about us. Blah, blah, blah. When I figured that out, I totally flipped. I mean, it sounded crazy. Dad? Dad's always been there for us. He's always loved us. And I told her she was obviously mistaken. But the second I said that, Gail turned on me. She told me I was naive. And she was really, really angry that I didn't believe her. She stormed out of my room and avoided me all night.

"By the time the party rolled around, I figured she

would be over it. I mean, this wasn't the first time this has happened between us. Moving in together in college maybe wasn't the best idea. Because we've had some disagreements. We haven't always seen eye to eye."

Claire gaped at her with confusion. Her daughters? Fighting throughout the semester? Hadn't she spoken to them numerous times on the phone? Hadn't they always indicated they were really happy?

Abby continued. "But she seemed even angrier than all those other times. Rachel and I were chasing her, trying to get her to talk to us, but she refused. She said, 'I'm done.'" Abby used air quotes, and her hands shook.

"Those were basically the last words she ever said to me. And I can't help but think it's all my fault," Abby rasped. "I pushed her away. I refused to listen. I mean, what she was saying really freaked me out. It didn't seem real. And it felt like an extension of all these other fights we'd had over the semester. I don't know. She was so dramatic lately. So different than she was here."

A feeling of dread stretched over Claire's chest, pressing against her heart. She gazed at her beautiful daughter, a creature so perfect she could hardly believe she'd once grown her in her body.

What was she saying? What was she alluding to?

"What did Gail mean about your father not caring about us? About him wanting to leave?" Claire rasped.

Abby raised her shoulders. "She never elaborated."

Claire stumbled back to the front desk of the flower shop, where she stared at the computer screen. What she read there looked like hieroglyphics rather than English.

"I mean, I've been too scared to tell you." Abby scrambled, her voice echoing between Claire's ears. "Because it's Dad. And I love Dad. But I just can't wrap my mind around this. Where did she go? And does it have something to do with what she was saying that night?"

Claire pressed her elbows on the front desk and closed her eyes. That night, Russel planned to return to Martha's Vineyard from his stint in the city. She'd already sent him photographs of the MISSING flyers, and he'd said: "Great idea. Let's hang more when I'm back." Were those the words of a man who had something to hide? Then again, they were just words. They meant nothing.

"Are you going to tell Dad about this?" Abby whispered. She sounded terrified.

"I don't know. I have to think," Claire said, surprising herself with how truthful she was. She no longer felt the inclination to lie to protect Abby.

"Is it because you think Dad had something to do with this?"

Claire closed her eyes. The earth beneath her tilted, and she swayed back and forth. From what seemed like a great distance, she heard Abby's voice, talking to someone else. "Yeah. Can you come pick us up, Aunt Charlotte? Mom's not feeling well." After that, she felt hands on her elbows and shoulders. She was guided to the chair in the back, where she sat with her eyes closed and her stomach simmering. She could have thrown up but didn't. Not long afterward, Charlotte arrived, feigning a smile. She helped Claire back outside, where snow was so thick, falling like a sheet. When Claire looked at her phone in Charlotte's car, she had another text from Russel.

> RUSSEL: I don't think I'll make it back
> tonight. The weather is too bad.
>
> RUSSEL: I'll try for tomorrow.

Claire breathed a sigh of relief. She wouldn't have to deal with that problem today. She could shelve it.

Back home, Rachel and Abby went upstairs, and Claire was too exhausted to chase them down and drag them back to the living room. Charlotte poured them glasses of Cab and sat with her on the couch, staring at her intently.

"I hope you know you can tell me anything," Charlotte said.

Claire rubbed her temples.

"I mean, I still remember how you were with me after Jason died." Charlotte continued. "You dragged me out of bed most days. You pushed me to build a new life. I wouldn't be with Everett if it wasn't for you. I'd probably still be in that bed down the road, nursing my wounds, thinking my life was over."

Claire shifted across the couch and laid her head on Charlotte's shoulder. "Apparently, Gail told Abby there was something up with Russel. And Abby got angry. That's why they were fighting."

Charlotte winced. "What was up with Russel?"

"Abby couldn't fully understand her," Claire explained. "She was crying too hard. But the gist is, I guess, that Russel isn't who he says he is. That he wants to leave us."

"Where did she get that idea?" Charlotte asked.

"No idea. Gail never clarified anything else." Claire took a long swig of wine and felt her anxiety drop. Bit by bit, reality was coming into focus. She filled her lungs with warm air.

"Are you going to approach Russel about this?"

"What could I say?" Claire began. "That Abby thinks

he might have something to do with her sister's disappearance? It sounds ridiculous."

"He probably didn't have anything to do with it," Charlotte reminded her. "But maybe Gail learned something about him. Something that drove her away."

Claire bit her bottom lip. Charlotte was the voice of reason, even if she really didn't want to hear what she had to say.

Finally, she spoke, and her voice was only a whisper. "Russel has been incredibly distant lately. I'm lonelier when he's here than when he's in the city."

Charlotte winced. "That's telling."

"But it's not like I want to leave him! No. Marriages go through peaks and valleys. Dynamics change."

"They do," Charlotte assured her, although her voice was edged with doubt.

Claire burrowed the back of her head against the couch cushion. Her heart thudded with a single thought. She couldn't lose both Russel and Gail in one fell swoop. That would be like getting her arm and leg chopped off at once. That would be like being buried alive.

Chapter Ten

Rina tapped her fingernail on the glass of Steve's rental vehicle, at first gently and then harder, until his eyes flickered open. He jumped with surprise, then raised his cap to peer out at her. His smile was crooked, his dimples sharp and deep, and Rina's stomach flipped over with recognition. Steve unlocked the door and stepped out, bringing with him that familiar smell—a mix of his auto shop and an expensive cologne that smelled of oak and leather. Rina held herself back from burrowing against him.

"What are you doing here?" Rina asked.

Steve closed the door of the car with a sharp click and took stock of their surroundings. The swell of blue sky and the little two-bedroom house Rina had called home for nearly ten years. It was bizarre to have him there in her world, so far from the one where they'd met. He didn't look from California in the slightest. His skin had paled since summer, and he still wore his coat.

"This is some place you have," Steve said. "Just a few

blocks from the beach! And that Pacific Ocean is gorgeous. So different from the Atlantic."

Rina shoved him gently, irritated that he'd ignored her question. It was easy to fall back into their old patterns and want to tease him again. "Come inside," she said, rolling her eyes. "You've had a long trip, I guess."

Steve collected his suitcase from the back and followed Rina into her house wordlessly. Rina racked her mind, trying to remember when she'd shared her address with Steve—and then remembered that his mother had asked for it because she'd wanted to send her a birthday card last year. That was probably how he'd gotten it.

Steve had tracked Rina down for a change. That was an invigorating feeling. Maybe it meant something.

Steve left his suitcase in the foyer and continued through to the kitchen, where Rina prepared a pot of coffee and crossed her arms over her chest. Seeing Steve so soon after walking past Penny's mural and sitting at the bedside of her very broken mother gave her whiplash. There were too many emotions at once.

"I like your kitchen," Steve began, his eyes tracing the red-painted walls, the linen curtains, the paintings Carmella had made and framed for her.

"It's small," Rina said. "Smaller than yours, anyway." After all, she hadn't raised children in this house. She hadn't needed anything more than one plate, one wine glass, one fork.

Steve nodded and shoved his hands in his pockets. Now that they were off his turf, Rina was seeing a side of him she never had before. He was earnest and nervous. "You didn't answer any of my phone calls."

Rina dragged her fingers through her bob. "It's been a really difficult time out here. I've been distracted."

Steve nodded. "How's your mom?"

"She doesn't remember what happened. She only remembers to hate me. And she's been using some very creative words to prove it."

Steve looked taken aback. Rina remembered that she hadn't told Steve any of her family history thus far. He'd probably assumed that Rina's parents were just as kind and loving as Trevor and Kerry Montgomery.

It was better not to assume anything. Rina had learned that in her line of work.

"Is Gail home?" Rina asked, pouring them both mugs of coffee.

"That's part of the reason I'm here," Steve said, his tone darkening. "She still hasn't turned up."

Rina frowned and slipped the pot back into the coffee maker. Steve's face was shadowed. Rina could feel the collective Montgomery family's heart breaking, even from a continent away. She could feel their panic, their devastation, and their desire to use anything and everything in their power to get Gail back.

She'd seen what missing children could do to the ones they'd left behind. She'd experienced it firsthand.

Rina led Steve back onto the porch, where they sat side-by-side on the swing, their eyes toward the glistening road. The chain clinked.

"She left her dorm room on January 6," Steve told her. "She hadn't spoken to her twin in about a week. They'd gotten into some kind of argument. I don't know the details."

Rina's heart felt bruised. The swing creaked beneath them, drawing them forth and back. "Claire must be out of her mind with worry." And then, it struck her. "Did she send you out here to find me?"

Steve shook his head. "No. This was all my idea." He winced, then added, "She did ask me to call. But this is what you do. It seemed obvious to ask for your advice."

Rina's stomach soured again. She took a big sip of coffee and reminded herself that her excitement for seeing Steve had been misplaced. Steve was here for her help—and that was fine. But he wasn't here because he wanted to be with her. Not the way she wanted him.

"In your experience," Steve asked, "why do young women like Gail run away?"

Rina puffed out her cheeks. "There are a few reasons. They feel misunderstood at home. They're in love with someone their parents don't approve of. They're into drugs and frightened of being caught. Then again, I've searched for what seems like hundreds of young women around Gail's age. The story is always slightly different."

"Meaning?"

"Meaning I don't want to assume anything regarding Gail's story," Rina said. "I don't want to do her that disservice. I'd need to know more about her case. About the people she hung out with. I'd need to talk to the twin. Abby's her name?"

Steve nodded. "I told Claire you have contacts. People you normally reach out to."

Rina's heart thumped. What else had she revealed to Steve over the past nine months of their friendship? She'd opened her heart to him in so many different ways, yet she'd neglected to tell him the things that really mattered. Was that the reason their intimacy had always felt so difficult to grasp?

"I have a few guys, sure," Rina said. "We might be able to see who she's messaging right now. If she wants to be found, she's probably texting all the time."

"If it's a cry for attention, you mean?"

"I guess so. If she really doesn't want to be found, there won't be anything." Rina's heartbeat quickened. She'd begun to fixate on the case, to shove her own problems aside and consider the emotional depths of this teenager she hardly knew.

"I know you're dealing with your own family stuff," Steve said quietly, putting his mug on the ground next to the swing. "I hope this isn't too much."

"She's your niece. And she needs my help. It's a done deal."

Rina palmed the back of her neck and swept her gaze to the Pacific, which looked like a long, glinting string on the horizon. She itched to walk along it, to feel the salty breeze on her cheeks. "Let's go," she said suddenly, traipsing off the porch swing. She went inside for a moment to fetch her keys and phone, then locked the house and led Steve down the block toward the water. They didn't speak; the only sound was the rush of cars as they swept past and their tennis shoes scuffing on the sidewalk. When they reached the beach, Rina removed her shoes and pressed her toes into the sand, thinking of it as a way of grounding herself and her emotions. Her heartbeat slowed.

"My sister disappeared, you know," Rina said, speaking to her toes rather than to Steve.

"Oh, Rina. Oh, I didn't know." Steve's voice was strained. He sat down on the sand next to her feet, and Rina collapsed beside him.

Before them, a toddler bubbled in and out of the sweeping water, his hand wrapped tightly around his mother's.

"She was fifteen," Rina said. "Normally, we walked

home from school together, but I had something to do that day, so she walked home alone. I didn't think anything of it. And when I got home, and she wasn't there, I still didn't think much of it. I was like, okay. Maybe she went to her boyfriend's house. Maybe she went to the gas station to buy an ice cream sandwich. Whatever. But the hours drifted forward, and she never came home."

Rina raised her chin to look at Steve, whose face was stricken. The sunlight had already worked its damage on his cheeks, tinging them red.

"My parents always blamed me for not walking her home that day," Rina said. "And when I became a private investigator, and I still hadn't found Penny? That made them hate me, I think."

"How could your parents hate you?" Steve whispered.

Rina wanted to laugh, but she kept it in. "Trust me. I've looked for her. I've used every resource I have. But whatever happened back in 1994 is not on any recording device. It's not written in any file. It's almost like my sister was never here at all." Rina swallowed. "I know what you're thinking. That my search for all these lost people is me, trying to make peace with the fact that I never found her. And you're right. But I still haven't found peace."

Steve placed his hand over Rina's on the sand. A shiver ran up and down her spine, even as she pulled her hand back and placed it on her lap. She couldn't deal with her emotions for Steve right now.

Sniffling, Rina took her phone from her pocket and wrote a few notes to her guys in the industry. She gave them Gail's name and information and asked for a full report of her social media files and texting. Although she'd only met one of the guys in person, she assumed they were all the same—computer-obsessed guys who liked to stay home and work cases like these.

"Okay," Rina said. "The guys have heard the call."

Steve shook his head, so that his curls ruffled over his ears. "Is it..." He trailed off. "I mean, what your guys do, digging around in internet files. Is it...?"

"Is it illegal, you mean?"

Steve raised his shoulders, looking sheepish.

"It is," Rina said. "Absolutely. But in this line of work, I've learned that I have to get my hands dirty. I do whatever I can to bring people home. It's so much better than the alternative— never seeing these people again. I mean, what's a few text messages when it comes to someone's life?"

Steve's eyes glowed. "I agree," he stuttered. "Thank you. Really. Claire will be so relieved you're working on this."

Rina imagined Claire at home, shivering as a Martha's Vineyard snow shot down outside. It was a different dimension to this sun-speckled California day.

Again, Steve reached for her hand, but Rina shook it off and set her jaw. Steve looked like a dog she'd just whacked over the nose.

"Steve," Rina began, her voice hollow. "I can't do this anymore."

Steve put his hand back on the sand slowly.

"It's just been in a gray area for too long." Rina continued. "And it hurts too much."

Steve dropped his chin to his chest and sighed deeply. The tension between them was so stiff; Rina felt she could pop it like a bubble. She touched his shoulder in a way she hoped was friendly, not romantic, and said, "But we're going to find Gail, okay? And we're going to stay friends."

Steve's eyes glinted. Rina wanted to scream at him, to tell him that his back-and-forth, will-they, won't-they parade had shattered her heart. But ultimately, the truth was far more complicated.

"You've been such a wonderful friend the past nine months," Rina breathed. "I needed a haven. Somewhere to hide from my life, from everything that happened with Penny and my parents, and everything that happened with Vic later on. I truly feel like a different person because of you."

It was bizarre to speak such truths to Steve. They'd waded around the truth since they'd met one another, neither willing to acknowledge it. But everything had to come into the light now. Now that they would be nothing to one another but friends.

Friendship was so important. Why did it always play second fiddle? Why was romantic love supposedly so much stronger?

"I understand. I really do," Steve said. He sounded like he had a frog in his throat, and his cheeks flashed crimson. "And you saved me from myself, too. More than you know."

Rina chuckled sadly. She had the urge to fall back on the sand and roll around, sobbing, like a woman who'd lost her mind.

"You should stay in California for a few days," she said, surprising herself. She genuinely didn't want him to leave yet. "You've never been here before. And I think you're due for a vacation."

"All those times I forced you to come out to Martha's Vineyard to see me, I could have been here in the sun."

But that wasn't the truth. In actuality, Rina had darted across the continent to Martha's Vineyard any chance she'd gotten. She'd probably forced herself on Steve, even when he hadn't wanted her. She'd tried to mold a romantic relationship out of nothing like some kind of fool.

"Come on," Rina said, popping up and dusting the sand from her pants. "I assume you're hungry?"

Steve laughed sadly. "Are you just saying that because I'm always hungry?"

"It's standard for you, Steve." Rina's smile felt made of plastic and apt to melt off her face. "There's a taco place just down the road. I should warn you, though. West Coast tacos are a different breed from East Coast ones. Prepare your palate for the experience of a lifetime."

Steve followed after her, and their shadows danced beside them, clambering over one another. In telling Steve what was on her mind, Rina felt a weight had been lifted from her chest. He understood how much she cared—and that she couldn't care this much anymore. It was destroying her.

Chapter Eleven

ong after Charlotte, Rachel, and Abby fell asleep that night, Claire tiptoed down the hall and crept into Russel's office. The clock on the wall read three thirty in the morning, but Claire felt starkly sober and more awake than ever.

Lying in the bed she shared with Russel had felt like floating in a poisonous lake. And she'd burned to know what Gail was referring to when she said Abby didn't know her father. What were Gail's secrets, wherever she was?

But Claire felt like a fish out of water in Russel's office. She only went in there to vacuum or put snacks on his desk, so much so that even the furniture and the decorations looked taken from somebody else's house. She hadn't had a hand in picking it out and couldn't even fathom where he'd purchased some of it. Certainly, it had come from off the island. She gripped the back of his desk chair, one of those meant to save your posture, closed her eyes, and tried to visualize Russel here; she tried to feel his thoughts as he entered this room every day. But nothing came to her.

Scared that someone would find her snooping, Claire closed the door and sat on the desk chair, surveying the landscape of Russel's things. It was a bit like digging through Gail's belongings in her dorm room, except for the fact that Russel was an entirely different breed. He was more organized than Gail. He liked to use his label machine and put the labels on various envelopes and folders. He liked to keep his computer keyboard dust-free. And he liked to use coasters for his coffee mugs and cans of late-afternoon beer, which he stacked in a precise line at the corner of the desk.

Russel had always been this organized, even back in high school. He'd been voted "Most Likely to Succeed" their senior year, making him feel crestfallen. *"I don't know what I want to succeed in,"* he'd told Claire privately. *"I feel like a failure just because everyone believes I'm about to do something grand."*

To this, Claire had said, *"You are going to do something grand. You're going to work for the city of Oak Bluffs. And you're going to marry me and have babies. What more could you want than that?"*

Russel had taken his laptop, his tablet, and both his work and personal phones with him to the city. This left his desktop. She tapped on the keyboard to wake up the screen. The background was a photograph of Gail and Abby on a recent vacation to Seattle, dressed in parkas that glinted with rain. Claire remembered the vacation well. It was their final trip as a family before Gail and Abby went off to college, and they'd spoken perpetually about their dreams for the future—about the classes they would take and the boys they would date and the parties they would attend. Nervous, Claire had given them a talking-to about drinking. "You're both lightweights, which means you just can't drink the way some other kids can. I beg you. Drink water. Pay attention to how you feel. And watch out for each other!"

Russel had later laughed with her about this in their private bedroom as another Seattle rain crashed outside their window. "They're going to make so many mistakes. That's what being eighteen is. And you have to let them, Claire."

Russel's computer was password protected, which felt bizarre. It wasn't like anyone else ever came into their house or entered Russel's office. Who was he protecting his files from?

Then again, Claire was pretty sure she'd read an article about thieves breaking into someone's house and stealing all of their bank information from their computer. Where had that happened? Ohio? Idaho? Maybe Russel was just being cautious. Protecting them. After all, the city council had already accused him of stealing from Oak Bluffs. Anything could happen.

But Claire couldn't help herself. She perched her fingers on the keyboard and typed the first thing that came to her mind—their wedding anniversary. It shook, indicating the password was false. After that, Claire tried Gail and Abby's birthday in July. Nope. Not that, either. Chewing on the inside of her cheek, she tried her birthday, Russel's birthday, Russel's parents' birthdays, followed by Russel's childhood pets' names, and on and on. She couldn't find it. And she'd begun to feel disgusted with herself, digging through her husband's computer like this.

Frustrated, she crossed her arms tightly and stared out

into the inky darkness beyond his office window. What else could she do? She could dig through Russel's files. She could tear apart the office closet. She could take a sledgehammer to his computer and go fully crazy. But none of it would bring Gail back.

Was it possible that Gail had misunderstood something? Claire's heartbeat slowed as she considered it. Maybe Gail had overheard a conversation Russel had with a client. Maybe he'd said something brash and stupid; something flirtatious. Gail was creative. Maybe she'd invented an entire world around a few words he'd said and decided to make a bigger deal out of it than it was.

That was a teenage girl's thing, right? Making a big deal out of nothing?

Claire walked back down the hall and collapsed in bed, no longer certain of anything. Gail's face floated in her mind's eye. As their mother, Claire had never had problems differentiating them. They'd always been unique to her. It had always seemed clear.

When Russel got home from the city the next day, Charlotte, Rachel, Abby, and Claire were at the coffee shop as a snowfall blustered outside the window. Claire had ordered a few slices of cake for the table, a carrot, a pistachio cream, and a cheesecake, but the four of them hardly picked at them, raising their forks and putting them back down again. It was January 12, six full days since Gail had left her dorm room and never returned. Time was having its way with them.

That was when the text from Russel came through.

RUSSEL: Where are you?

Claire's heartbeat intensified. Russel had said he was coming home today, but she'd half believed he wouldn't make it, that he'd find a reason to stay in New York City.

"Your father's back," Claire said to Abby.

Abby's cheeks were pale. She sipped her coffee and said, "You aren't going to tell him what I told you. Are you?"

"No," Claire assured her. *Not yet.*

Charlotte and Rachel had decided to stay with Trevor and Kerry while Russel was at the house. "You need your space," Charlotte said. "And Mom has been texting me nonstop since we got back, demanding we come over. You'd think I wasn't just here for the holidays."

Claire and Abby hugged Charlotte and Rachel close and abandoned their uneaten slices of cake, tumbling back into the frigid air. Claire drove Abby back home wordlessly. The car filled with the sense of dread. But when the garage door lifted, Russel opened the adjoining door immediately and smiled warmly at them. He wore his house clothes, sweatpants and a sweatshirt, and his hair was ruffled and wild without his normal mousse. More than anything, he looked worried, his eyes bloodshot.

Claire removed her boots and stepped into his arms. He smelled the same as he always had.

"I don't know what I thought," Russel breathed into her ear. "When you weren't here. I was worried I'd lost all of you."

Claire felt his heartbeat through his sweatshirt. Tears sprung to her eyes.

"There's my girl," Russel said, extending an arm toward Abby. Abby hurried to join their group hug, and

Russel held them there, sturdy as a rock, as the winter winds rocketed against the house.

Claire was suddenly ravenous. In the kitchen, she scraped butter over slices of rye bread and made everyone toasted ham-and-cheese sandwiches with cheddar melting out the sides. Russel and Abby sat on the stools of the kitchen island, Russel with a beer and Abby with a green juice. There was a heaviness in the space where Gail should have been.

Was this their new normal?

After they ate, Abby excused herself upstairs to attend an online class. Rina scrubbed the skillet as Russel cracked another beer. He was often riled up after the city; the stress from all those meetings and important people sent his blood pressure skyrocketing.

"Steve's in California," Claire heard herself say. "He told me Rina reached out to some of her contacts. People who might be able to figure out what Gail was up to before she left."

Russel's face turned a soft shade of green. "That's great."

Claire dried her hands on a kitchen towel and gazed at Russel. Her heart thudded with love for him. She prayed he wouldn't sense she'd been in his office, snooping. She prayed everything was in precisely the same place.

"Steve said we should try to think of everything Gail might have mentioned to us." Claire continued. "Rina says every detail could be important. Even the ones we don't think are anything special."

Russel scratched his beard, his eyes toward the window. Another few inches of snow had already fallen just that afternoon. "Gosh, babe. I can't think of anything special."

Claire's heart sank. "Abby said something about a fight they had before the New Year's Eve party."

Russel arched his brow.

"And apparently, they weren't getting along that well throughout the semester."

"That's pertinent," Russel said. "Don't you think?" Color began to return to Russel's cheeks.

"It doesn't change the fact that we don't know where she is."

"But it means she had reason to leave," Russel said. "It means her sister had something to do with it."

Claire bristled. "This isn't Abby's fault."

"I didn't say that." Russel took a long slug from his beer, and his Adam's apple bounced up and down. "I just mean that something happened between them. And Gail is acting out."

Claire hung the skillet back on the kitchen rack and watched Russel, her distrust mounting. Why was he so eager to pin the blame on Abby?

"Are you back for a while?" Claire asked. "It would be nice to have you here. Abby and I haven't been doing so well."

Something like sorrow flickered across Russel's face. "I wish I could, babe. I really do. But this account is giving me a heart attack. Randall needs me back in a few days. Hopefully not as long this time."

Claire's lips fell into a line.

"I can't put my entire career on hold right now," Russel continued, his voice edged with anger. "You know that. You know all I've worked for."

Claire knew there was no arguing with him. She peered at him through the slits of her eyes.

Russel walked around her, set his beer on the counter, and wrapped his hands around her shoulders. He began to knead the knots in her back, which were strained and tight after a week of tension and fear. Even as he rotated the muscle, Claire couldn't loosen up, not like she once had. She stared out the window as Russel told her to calm down, calm down, and wondered if she'd been living with a monster all this time.

Chapter Twelve

Rina woke up at five thirty, put on her running gear, and stepped into the shadows of the hallway, pushing her earbuds into her ears. The coffee pot gurgled from the kitchen, and Rina was grateful for the sound, even with all the baggage it brought. She wasn't alone in this house all by herself, like always. Someone was here to greet the morning with her.

"You're up early," Rina said.

Steve stood in a pair of sweatpants and a white undershirt, gripping the handle of a coffee mug and leaning against the kitchen counter. Rina had told him to help himself to whatever he wanted. He'd slipped into her life easily. That said, she'd meant what she'd said about their "romance" being over. She'd asked him to sleep in the guest bedroom—just one room away from where Rina had tossed and turned.

"I'm still three hours ahead," Steve said groggily. "It's eight thirty for me."

Rina poured herself a mug of coffee and removed her earbuds. The run could wait. "I have to visit my mother today. Visiting hours start at ten. I guess I'll stay till noon or so."

"Do you want me to come with you?"

Rina winced. "I don't know why you would." Steve was just a friend. She didn't want to over-complicate things or confuse her amnesia-ridden mother even more. She didn't want Steve to start to think he owed her anything.

"But we can get brunch after," Rina added. "I know a good place in Venice."

"Venice Beach?" Steve's eyes lit up.

"The very same."

Rina went for a run alone, trying to shove her thoughts of Steve, Gail's disappearance, and her mother's accident into the back corners of her mind. Her muscles screamed as she got faster, faster, charging down the boardwalk as though someone was chasing her. When she got back home, she was slick with sweat, and Steve's eyes lit up even more—proof that he was attracted to her. But attraction had never been the problem between them.

Rina drove to the hospital and found her father, Wally, downstairs with a cup of coffee, chatting with another older man whose wife, apparently, was staying in the same ward as Ellen.

"We grew up down the block from each other," Wally announced to Rina. "And we never even met!"

Rina stuck out her hand. "I'm his daughter."

"Penny, right?" The man's smile showed that he'd lost several teeth on the righthand side. "Your father has told me so much about you."

Rina couldn't breathe for a moment. She had no idea her father just casually mentioned Penny's name like that; talking about her as though she'd just gone across the road to buy a carton of milk. Wally didn't seem to notice. Instead, he said, "This is my other daughter. Rina. She's a detective. Sort of like Sherlock Holmes."

The man's eyes sparkled. Rina suddenly felt very dirty. "I'm going upstairs," she said. "See you later."

As Rina walked down her mother's hallway, she breezed past Dr. Bartlett, then stumbled backward and called his name. "Excuse me?"

Dr. Bartlett gave her a sleepy smile. "Good morning. I was just with your mother. She's still confused, but she's healing well."

"That's great. Thank you." Rina's heart skipped a beat. "I wondered if you could tell me something."

"Sure thing."

"Where did the ambulance pick my mother up? After the accident, I mean."

Dr. Bartlett nodded and beckoned for a passing nurse. He asked her to access Ellen's file and pass along this information to her daughter. Rina thanked him and followed the nurse, who slipped the file into her hands without a second glance. Being related to someone, it seemed, allowed you unlimited access to information. As a private investigator who often had to go to great lengths to get information, this was a completely different game.

According to the report, the ambulance picked Ellen and Wally up at the side of the busy road near the beach. In it, Wally was reported as saying he'd tried to carry Ellen to their car before losing energy and needing assistance. This boggled Rina's mind. Her father had tried to carry her mother? Despite broken bones? Despite blood?

The accident had happened early in the morning on New Year's Eve—six thirty, in fact. That meant Wally hadn't contacted Rina about the incident until hours later. Had she been an afterthought to him? Had he jolted awake at the hospital and remembered, "Oh, yes. Our other daughter should know about this?"

But the fact that Wally had moved her after the accident begged the question: where had the incident happened? Had there been any witnesses? Had someone seen Wally attack Ellen?

Rina thanked the nurse and proceeded into her mother's hospital room. Ellen was awake, watching a soap opera on the television. Using her good hand, she dug through a bowl of oatmeal and fruit and ate slowly, as though chewing irritated the bruises on her jaw.

"Oh, Mom," Rina breathed. "What happened to you?"

Ellen turned to look at Rina curiously. Then she said, "You know, I think he's cheating on her."

Rina blinked. "Excuse me?"

Ellen gestured toward the television with her spoon. "I think he's cheating. You can see it in his eyes when he talks to her. She shouldn't trust him. I wouldn't. You know, your father never cheated on me. Not in almost fifty years of marriage. We were always in love. Always." Ellen spooned another bit of oatmeal and chewed gingerly. "And most married couples can't say that, you know. Most everyone divorces. You divorced. Remember, Rina?"

"Yes, Mom."

"We never liked that Vic." Ellen went on, not looking at Rina. "Maybe we should have said something before you went ahead and married him. I don't know."

Well, Rina thought to herself. At least her memory is coming back to her. Slowly.

It made sense that she brought up the dark parts first. That was how Ellen's brain operated. Maybe she'd already obliterated the lighter parts, the happier days of Rina's life.

Rina sat on the plastic chair by her mother's bed and watched the soap opera for a while. It was true what her mother said, that she was pretty sure the main guy was cheating on his fiancée. But the fiancée wasn't totally without blame, either. She was having an intense emotional affair with her ex-boyfriend from high school, a science teacher who often spoke in science-related riddles. Rina was embarrassed to admit she got wrapped up in the soap opera story. She tried to guess what might happen next—where the twisted minds of the writers were going. When her father came in with another cup of coffee and sat with them, Ellen shushed him and said she was "watching her stories with her daughter." Rina was again embarrassed to admit her mother's desire to spend time with Rina pleased her, even if they weren't speaking.

After visiting hours, Rina and Wally walked downstairs and said goodbye without hugging. Just before she left, Rina asked, "And you're sure Mom just fell down like that? While she was walking?"

Wally sputtered, "What else could have happened?"

Rina sighed. She didn't want to get into it. Not now. Not when she didn't have more proof. "All right, Dad."

Besides, did she really want to put her father in prison? What was her plan?

Rina returned home to pick up Steve, who'd showered and changed into jeans and a V-neck T-shirt. He was already tanned from his two days in California and spoke at length about a podcast he'd listened to while doing sit-ups—something about modernized auto shops. Rina half listened, her mind still on her mother.

The brunch place in Venice was packed to the gills. Rina and Steve waited outside for fifteen minutes, studying the menu and watching Venice locals along the boardwalk.

"It looks like everyone is here to show off," Steve said under his breath.

Rina knew what he meant. Roller skaters breezed past in sparkly outfits, showing too much skin, dancers performed together in troupes, and men walked shirtless with surfboards, their washboard abs glistening.

"It's a different world," Steve finished. "None of these people have even seen the East Coast before."

"I imagine you're right."

The server showed them to an outdoor table, where Steve ordered eggs Benedict and coffee, and Rina ordered a stack of pancakes with berries and a cappuccino. She was famished.

"How did it go today?" Steve asked, sounding nervous.

Rina raised her shoulders. "Mom's healing okay. Her memory seems to be slowly coming back. And she's fixated on a soap opera, which is keeping her brain active, at least."

"It's terrible to see a parent in the hospital like that," Steve said.

"Right," Rina remembered. "Your father had that horrible accident a few years back."

"It was awful. Then again, I'll always remember that it brought my little brother, Andy, back to the island."

"After so many years away," Rina said. She felt as though she could write a biography of Steve's life.

Yet he'd hardly scratched the surface of hers.

"How did your mom fall?" Steve asked.

Rina's shoulders fell forward. "That's a complicated question."

"What do you mean?"

Rina explained what she'd learned about the accident. That her mother's bruises and broken bones didn't align with her father's story. That her father carried her as far as he could before the ambulance came.

"But my father, for all his faults, was never abusive," Rina went on. "Avoidant? Yes. Hardly home? Yes. But I've never seen him raise a hand to anyone."

"I'm so sorry you're going through this." Steve shook his head. "Is there anything I can do?"

Rina wanted to laugh. "Can you build a time machine and take me back?"

"I'll do my best."

Rina's face fell with shame. She knew that mentioning the past was a difficult thing with Steve. He would have taken himself back to when Laura was alive, and Rina and Steve didn't even know one another's names.

Rina's phone dinged with a message from her contact, one of the guys she'd put on the case to dig through Gail's messages. He'd sent her the files of messages from social media accounts and her phone number.

"Hey, Rina! Here are the files you asked for. At first glance, Ms. Gail seems like a typical teenager—gossiping with friends, sending memes, and flirting with boys. The whole gamut. You'll see numerous text messages between her and a guy named Nathan Rodgers, who seems to have been a love interest since October. As we both know, nine times out of ten, these missing young folks run away with a romantic partner. I would start there."

Rina turned the phone so Steve could read. Light returned to his eyes.

"Nathan Rodgers," he read aloud. "He already sounds slimy!"

"We can't assume anything right now," Rina said. She'd followed too many leads that had gone nowhere to allow herself even a slice of hope.

Rina downloaded the enormous file and hurried to read the most recent messages from Gail, hoping there were a few from after her January 6 disappearance. Maybe she'd assumed nobody would be able to access her files. Maybe she'd given herself away.

"Oh," Rina breathed.

"What's up?" Steve looked stricken.

Rina gestured toward her phone. "Gail only sent a few messages after January 6. And none of them give any kind of clue about where she is or what's on her mind." Her heart thudded with dread.

"What do they say?"

"One seems to be to a female friend, and it says, 'I left all my Jane Austen books in my room; you can go through them if you want.' Another is to the same friend and says, 'Abby can be such a snake.' And the last one is written to another female friend and says, 'I mean, I'm an adult now. I have to act like it.' But they dry up by January 9. Maybe whoever she was with told her to stop sending messages altogether."

Steve furrowed his brow. "Or maybe they forced her to stop. Maybe this Nathan kid stole her phone."

Rina's heart pounded. "One thing we can confirm is

that Gail knew she was going away. She wanted to give her friend her books. She wanted to act like an adult."

"Why is it that young people think they're adults the minute they hit eighteen?" Steve asked.

Rina sipped her cappuccino, remembering her own past—how she'd thrown herself into the abyss of adulthood as quickly as she could. How she'd ached to get away from her parents as quickly as possible. How she'd blamed herself for her sister's disappearance, poisoning her soul in the process.

"What should we do now?" Steve asked.

"You need to call Claire and ask her about this Nathan guy," Rina said, forcing herself back to the current reality. "He's our best bet right now to find Gail."

"Read the messages she wrote to Nathan," Steve ordered. "Maybe they'll give us a clue."

But when Rina pulled up Nathan's file, she found nothing but an embarrassing display of heart-on-their-sleeves affection, the sort that only teenagers were capable of, because they didn't yet know the cruelty of the world. Gail sent numerous selfies, heart emoji, kiss emoji, and memes that expressed how much she was thinking about him. It seemed the two of them had met in early October and begun a sizzly affair—one that probably consisted of a lot of dates at the university dining hall.

"Did Gail ever have any high school boyfriends?" Rina asked, just as the server arrived with their platters of food. The steam from her pancakes filled the air between them.

"No," Steve said, unrolling his napkin from his fork and knife and gazing across the ocean. "I remember Isabella talking about it. About how Gail, Abby, and Rachel never branched out from one another. She was afraid for them, wondering what would happen when they got to college and were forced to grow up." Steve sniffed. "But she never could have envisioned this."

"Nobody could have," Rina agreed. "But we're getting closer to finding her."

Rina wanted to tell Claire it would be all right—but she began to have doubts about that. False hope was the worst kind of poison.

Chapter Thirteen

Claire was at her mother and father's when Steve called her about Nathan Rodgers. Standing in the sunroom with the phone pressed hard against her ear, she listened intently. Beside her was the Christmas tree her mother kept up all through January. Out the window, snow swelled over the sand dunes, and the ocean lapped against the sands. It all looked so ordinary.

"You're telling me Gail had a boyfriend?"

"That's right," Steve said. "Rina suggests you talk to Abby about him. I'm sure she'll know who he is."

"Why didn't Abby bring this up already?" Claire rasped, careful not to speak too loudly. Abby was in the kitchen with Kerry, washing dishes from lunch. She could hear the patter of their voices through the hall.

"Maybe they broke up," Steve said.

"Do the messages indicate that?"

"The messages between Gail and Nathan end on January 3," Steve explained. "Three days before she went missing."

"So that means they weren't talking when she left?"

"Rina thinks it's possible they already had a plan in place," Steve said. "Maybe they stopped communicating via text message just in case anyone was reading. Like us."

The premeditation Steve and Rina suggested boggled Claire's mind. Getting Gail to do her homework before the due date had been hard enough.

She must have really wanted to go.

"But none of the messages talk about Gail and Abby's fight on New Year's Eve?"

"None," Steve affirmed sadly. "I'm sorry."

Steve agreed to send along the file of messages just in case anything triggered Claire's memory. Just before they got off the phone, Claire remembered to ask, "How is California?"

"It's okay," Steve said. He sounded sad. "I'm getting a nice tan."

Claire wasn't in the right place to dig deeper into her brother's psyche. That had to come later—after Gail was found. She sighed. "Take care of yourself, Steve. I love you."

"I love you, too."

Claire clutched her phone to her chest, took a deep breath, and called Abby's name. She was reminded of crying out her girls' names for dinner when they'd been upstairs together, playing with Barbies, falling through imaginative worlds.

Abby appeared a moment later, her eyes shadowed. She strung her skinny arms together, putting up what seemed to be a classic teenage wall. "What's up?"

"Could you sit down, please?" Claire gestured toward the chair opposite the couch along the wall, the one nearest the window. She wanted to look her daughter head-on; she wanted to study the glint in her eyes, to look for potential clues. Ultimately, she wanted to see if her daughter was lying. She couldn't rule anything out anymore.

Claire sat across from her daughter, her palms flat on her thighs, and decided to just come out with it. "Do you know someone named Nathan Rodgers?"

Abby flinched as though she'd been smacked. It was clear she knew him.

"How did you...?" Abby stuttered.

Claire raised her hand to stop her. "Just tell me who he is." She sounded formal, as though she conducted a job interview or a police investigation.

Abby pulled her hair, and her eyes glinted. "Ugh. I hate that guy." Abby's words held a surprising amount of vitriol behind them.

"Abby. Come on." Claire wanted to scream. "Tell me who he is."

"Nathan is a master's student at the University of Massachusetts," Abby explained. "He's studying literature."

"Master's student?"

"Yeah. He's like twenty-three or something," Abby sniffed. She said "twenty-three" as though it were as old as fifty-five.

"And he knows Gail?"

"We technically met him on the same night. I guess that was late September or early October," Abby said. "It's totally rare to get invited to a house party off-campus as a freshman, but my friend Tiff's brother has a house, and we ended up there one night. It was like a college party you see in the movies. Gail was so impressed."

Claire's brain twisted with technicolor fears. She imagined her darling twins drinking disgusting cans of domestic beer around men as old as twenty-three. She imagined them doing things they regretted or didn't remember. Her heart felt heavy.

"And Nathan was there?"

"Yeah. He's friends with Tiff's brother, somehow."

"Tell me everything, Abby," Claire ordered. "Everything he said when you met him."

Abby's eyes widened. "You think Nathan took Gail?"

"I don't know. I don't know." Claire could have repeated this mantra forever until she went crazy with it.

Abby folded her lips. "Gail and I were with Tiff on the couch, listening to music and talking."

"Did you have anything to drink?"

"Mom. Of course." Abby shot Claire a look. "But not very much, okay?"

Claire filled her lungs with air and told herself not to freak out.

"Tiff's brother came over to us to make sure we were okay. We were the youngest people there, and he was being protective. Nathan wasn't far away, and he started teasing Tiff's brother about it. I remember one of us shot back at Nathan. It could have been any of us. But after that, Nathan came over and started chatting us up. Because he was a master's student in literature, Gail latched onto him pretty quickly. You know how she is with books."

Claire did know. Gail was obsessive when it came to reading. Ever since she'd learned, she'd been up to her ears in different stories, frequently packing an entire backpack of books for vacation.

"Anyway, Tiff and I got bored with all the book talk

and left them to it for a while," Abby said. "And when I got back to check on her, they were making out."

Claire's stomach curdled. In her mind, twenty-three might as well have been one hundred years older than Gail's eighteen. Maybe Nathan Rodgers was a predator?

But no. Gail was eighteen. She was in college. She was remarkably intelligent for her age, and she'd probably read more books than Claire had—an embarrassing fact that also left Claire giddy with pride for her daughter. She was probably more than Nathan's academic equal.

"Did she go home with him?" Claire asked in a small voice.

Abby shook her head. "No way! I wouldn't let her. But she was really angry with me about that. All the way home, she told me she'd never felt this way. That she'd finally met someone. That she finally understood all that 'love stuff' she'd read about in books." Abby shook her head. "I figured he wouldn't call her after that. That's what guys do, right? They get tired of you quickly. But Nathan texted her the next day and asked what she was up to. Gail went out to dinner with him and started hanging out with him all the time. Like, all the time, Mom. And it looked like they were headed toward happily ever after."

Abby stuttered and wrapped her hand around her neck. "I mean, I wasn't really pleased about this. I hardly saw Gail for a couple of months. And I really missed her, you know. And I admit. I was a little bit jealous. Gail swept into college and got an older boyfriend like that." Abby snapped her fingers. "And I was just going on terrible dates with nineteen-year-olds with pimples and pizza breath. When Gail was around, I picked fights with her. I told her that Nathan wasn't right for her. And I told her that he'd get bored with her because he knew so many older women and stuff."

Abby's cheeks were as white as the snow that swirled outside. "I'm not proud of any of this. And I totally see how I created a rift between Gail and me. It was so bizarre to fight with her. We'd never really done it before, and I think we both said some things we can't take back." Abby hung her head. "Especially now."

Claire's heart felt bruised. This was too much information at once. She felt as though she'd pull back the curtain on her daughters' lives and seen more than she'd planned for.

"Anyway, I assumed Nathan and Gail broke up in early December," Abby said. "I never saw him around the dorms anymore, and Gail spent more and more time at home. Things were actually good between us for the first time in a while. I decided not to ask about Nathan. I wanted to pretend he didn't exist."

Abby planted her palm on her forehead and looked out the window. She looked far older than her eighteen years, as though time and grief had crept up and aged her considerably. She needed her other half.

"I don't understand, Abby," Claire whispered. "Why didn't you ever mention Nathan? Gail's been missing for over a week, and he never came up. Not once."

Abby flinched and dropped her chin. She looked as though she wanted to fold her arms and limbs up and hide herself away.

"Gail is still my best friend. My twin," she said carefully. "She didn't want to tell you guys about Nathan, and I wanted to respect that. Besides, like I said, I thought they were broken up. I was so grateful not to have to think about him anymore."

"Are you sure that's everything?" Claire asked, sounding accusatory.

"That's all I can remember about Nathan."

"Did you ever go to his house? Do you know where he lives?"

Abby shook her head. "Somewhere off campus. But I never went there with Gail."

Claire searched her gut for some sense that Abby had omitted anything. She'd already trickled her facts slowly, revealing the story to be an onion. After a deep well of silence, Abby forced her eyes back to her mother.

"Did you ask Dad about what Gail said?"

Claire hesitated before she shook her head. She felt like a coward.

"Good," Abby breathed. Relief flowed through her face.

Claire wasn't sure what Abby meant by that. Before she could ask, Rachel hurried down the hallway to find her, her hair flowing out behind her. Abby looked at Rachel as though she were a lifeline.

"There you are," Rachel said.

Abby's eyes begged for release. Claire tilted her head, and Abby burst from the sunroom chair, grabbed Rachel's hand, and headed upstairs. As they went, Abby's whisper echoed through the stairwell, filling Rachel in on Nathan Rodgers. Claire felt tremendously tired, as though her arms and legs were filled with lead.

Before she returned to her mother in the kitchen, Claire got up the nerve to call the university and inquire about Nathan Rodgers. But the woman who answered could give her very little information. "I can't give you any details about Nathan, other than the fact that he no longer attends the University of Massachusetts," she said. "He dropped out in December."

"Right before finals?" Claire asked, perplexed.

"It's possible he wasn't prepared or thought he would fail anyway," the woman said breezily. "These kids drop out for all kinds of reasons."

Claire had hit a wall. She thanked the woman and hung up.

Chapter Fourteen

Rina returned from her run to find Steve on the front porch swing in his sweats, drinking coffee and reading a book. His face was serene, and he was barefoot, his toes shifting gently on the ground as he swung back and forth. She felt a wave of tenderness for him, for all they'd gone through together—and resisted the temptation to rush up the porch steps, throw her arms around him, and kiss him on his plump, wonderful lips.

Instead, she waved hello, breezed back through the house, poured herself a cup of coffee, and joined him on the swing with a book. It was pleasant to feel the sweat on her arms and legs dry, leaving a crisp layer of salt. The temperature was still in the sixties, and a blanket of clouds crept toward them, stretching over the sterling-blue sky.

Despite the chaos of the world and all that Rina didn't understand, she felt serene in a way she hadn't ever felt in her house alone. She could practically feel the sturdy beat of Steve's heart just a foot away. It was grounding.

It would be difficult to find a man like Steve, Rina knew. But she had to try. Eventually. When she got up the energy to date again.

"What's your plan today?" Rina asked, hating to break the smooth air between them.

Steve set down his book and sipped his coffee. "Depends on your plans, I guess." His eyes sparkled. "Are you going to visit your mother?"

"Not till this afternoon," Rina said. "And afterward, I was thinking of asking my father out to dinner. Maybe, if I get him at a table, I can pester him for details about my mother's accident. Maybe he'll have nowhere to run?"

"You're crafty," Steve said.

Rina tilted her head, her thoughts spinning. "Actually, maybe you should come, too."

"Really?"

"Yeah. I think you'd throw him off a little," Rina said. "He'll try to impress you and be all over the place."

"Okay. You're craftier than I thought. I'm in." Steve frowned, then added, "Do you want me to pretend to be something? Like, I don't know. Your boyfriend?"

Rina winced. She felt the question like a knife through her stomach.

Still, it made sense. If Wally thought Steve was a potential incoming member of the family, perhaps he'd open up more. Perhaps he'd want to talk "man to man."

"If you feel comfortable doing that," Rina said. "I don't want to pressure you."

"It's not a big deal," Steve said. "We've practically been doing that in front of my family for the past nine months."

Rina pulled her feet onto the swing and wrapped her

arms around her legs, forming into a ball. She decided to ignore this comment because it hurt too deeply to acknowledge it.

"Have you heard from Claire?"

Steve nodded. "She sent me loads of messages last night. Apparently, Nathan was Gail's boyfriend. Abby's pretty sure they broke up, but Gail never mentioned it, and Abby didn't pry. Abby wasn't too fond of Nathan."

Rina groaned. "And what does Abby think of the theory that Nathan had something to do with Gail's disappearance?"

"I don't know," Steve admitted. "We'll have to call her later. After dinner, maybe."

"After dinner," Rina agreed.

When Wally learned that Rina had a boyfriend from out East, his eyes sparkled with intrigue. "A boyfriend? I never thought you'd try again with that whole thing. That makes me happy."

Rina supposed "that whole thing" meant romance, companionship, starting again. She decided not to take issue with the flippant way he referred to her life, not now. There were bigger fish to fry.

They stood in the bottom hallway of the hospital, with its glowing white walls, its linoleum recently mopped. It was impossible to know how many lives had been destroyed in this very building and how much bad news had been received. Rina set her jaw. Her mother was healing—but she still hadn't mentioned anything to do with the accident. Wally knew something; there was a darkness behind the sparkle of his eyes.

"He wants to meet you," Rina continued.

"And I'd love to meet him, too. It's not every day your forty-five-year-old daughter has a new boyfriend."

Rina's stomach curdled. "Dinner? Tonight?"

"You name the place and time, and I'll be there."

Rina returned home to find Steve in the backyard, watering her flowers with a long green hose. He looked so casual back there, as though he'd always lived in that house with her, as though his toes were accustomed to walking across that lush grass. She waved from the kitchen window and drank an entire glass of water as her heart pounded in her ears. Again, she wondered if her father had hurt her mother? What would she do? And again, she figured she would cross that bridge when she came to it.

Steve dressed in the outfit Rina had purchased for him on the way back from the hospital: a white button-down and a pair of slacks. He showed it off, twisting his hips like a model as he strutted. "My father would be ashamed," he joked. "I've gone full Californian."

"You're playing a part tonight," Rina explained. "You have to look like the kind of man my father could see me with. And my father is pure Californian, going back generations. This is all he understands."

"Should I speak differently?" Steve asked. "All you Californians say 'dude' a lot, right?"

Rina rolled her eyes and laughed. "Don't lean too far into the stereotypes. You don't want to offend him. He's a Stanford graduate, remember."

"And I'm just a car mechanic from out East," Steve said. "But I reckon he can't fix his own Porsche."

"Lamborghini," Rina corrected. "And no. He can't."

Steve drove his rental car to the fish restaurant on the

outskirts of Santa Monica, where the land pulled away from the Eastern Coast to present a gorgeous view of the Ferris wheel and the boardwalk beyond. It was seven thirty, and the sky was a blistering shade of pink and orange.

"It's like a dream," Steve said as they headed up the walkway to the beachside restaurant.

"Or a nightmare," Rina said.

Wally was already at the restaurant, standing near their table and chatting up the server as though they'd known one another for years. When he spotted Steve, his eyes lit up, and he beelined for him with his hand extended. Rina knew what her father was thinking. Steve was handsome and looked accomplished. He could brag about him to his friends later. He fit the part.

Rina ordered a bottle of rosé and sparkling water for the table. She sat next to Steve on one side, across from her father, who donned his sunglasses and gazed, captivated, at the sunset.

"You have sunsets like this out East, Steve?" Wally asked.

"We're more in the sunrise business," Steve said.

Wally cackled and clapped the table with his palm. Rina gave Steve a small smile. He was buttering him up. The rosé would help, too. And just as Rina had suspected, Wally seemed less interested in learning about Steve than blabbering about his own life. Rina had recently read the definition of "narcissist" and seen both her mother's and father's faces floating in her mind's eye.

Over rosé, Wally talked about anything and everything that came to mind. He spoke about his business, which he'd recently sold in a healthy, multimillion-dollar sale. He mentioned Ellen frequently, as though she was just in the bathroom and poised to return to the table any moment. And he spoke of Rina here and there, too, knowing that he had to in order to relate to Steve. That was why they were both here, after all. Rina had brought them together.

They ordered fish for dinner—lobster, clams with spaghetti, and salmon plus noodle dishes, fresh bread, and salads. They shared everything as though they were a part of a different type of family. As though they were like the Montgomerys, who so often dined that way, passing plates around the table, cracking jokes, picking up where they'd left off the last time they'd had dinner.

Rina could see it in Steve's eye that he didn't trust her father. He'd already picked up on the difference between Wally and Trevor. But Steve had a way with people, probably from his years in the auto industry, talking to every type of person under the sun.

After they cleaned their plates, Rina elbowed Steve gently. It was time.

"Well, I'm sorry Ellen couldn't join us tonight," Steve said, smiling. "But Rina says she's healing up pretty well?"

Wally's expression deflated. "The doctors say she'll be there a bit longer. I'm hoping we can get her home by the end of February. But who knows? She took a bad tumble."

Already, this verbiage felt different to what Wally had said at the hospital.

"That sounds terrifying," Steve said, furrowing his brow, showing empathy. "I watched my mother go down a few years ago, and the memory of it kept me awake at night."

Wally's eyes glinted. He returned his gaze to the horizon, where the sun had completely disappeared. Night drenched everything, casting ghoulish shadows along the beach. "You can't imagine what it was like. I watched the love of my life fall away from me. And there was nothing I could do."

It was as though Wally had forgotten Rina was there at all. His eyes remained focused on Steve.

Under his breath, he rasped, "I can't help but blame myself. Even though she hit me first. She lost her balance a split-second later, and I couldn't grab her in time." Wally imitated it, throwing his hand forward and then falling back against the chair. "You should have seen the way she fell down those stairs. She looked like a rag doll. I ran after her and tried to carry her back to the car. My darling bride. My love."

Rina's heart pounded. She could imagine it even though it hurt. Her frail mother teetering back like that.

"Why did she hit you?" Steve whispered.

Wally spread his fingers out on the tablecloth and stared down at them as though he wasn't sure they were his. "I told her something. Something that really upset her."

This was it, Rina thought. Maybe her father had cheated on her mother. Maybe he'd revealed a second family, another life, the ultimate betrayal of many decades of lies. As a private investigator, she'd seen it all. She couldn't be surprised anymore.

"Our daughter, Penny, is alive," Wally said softly. "After thirty years away, she contacted me."

Rina's mouth went dry. She felt like she was floating.

But Wally wasn't done.

"I'd waited a full month before I told Ellen about

Penny. You can imagine how much that hurt her, realizing I'd carried that with me. That's why she hit me. The reveal was enormous. She hated me for covering it up."

Chapter Fifteen

Gail's high school classmates posted photographs of Gail on their social media. "Have you seen this girl? She's missing! Help us find her!" Claire swiped past their posts through photographs of Gail in many awkward stages of high school, remembering birthday parties, theater productions, and marching band parades. In one of the photos, Gail's friend Bianca wrapped her arms around both Gail and Abby in front of the Sunrise Cove. It had to have been their fifteenth birthday— so many eons ago. If Claire remembered correctly, that had been when Zach had ruined Christine's perfectly decorated cake. Not long afterward, Christine and Zach had fallen in love.

Russel returned home after two days in the city. Claire heard the garage door purr up and set her tablet to the side. She realized she'd been scrolling through social media posts for hours, looking for clues about where Gail could be. She'd even looked for Nathan, but it seemed he didn't have a social media account. Abby suggested he was "too cool" for an online presence. Claire had no idea what she meant.

Russel breezed into the house, placed his suitcase by the door, and opened the fridge. Claire listened to the familiar rhythm. Soon, he would exit the kitchen and find her in front of the crackling fire, looking in a sorry state. She wore no makeup, and she hadn't washed her hair in days. Her thought, always, was: what if Gail called while she was washing her hair? What if she couldn't hear?

"Oh! Hey. There you are." Russel greeted her from the doorway between the kitchen and living room. He was eating a slice of cold pizza, dressed in what looked to be an exquisite suit. Claire hadn't had anything to do with its purchase. Once upon a time, Russel had struggled knowing what color combinations to put together. Now, he had a business-savvy wardrobe.

"Hey. How was the city?" Claire's voice cracked.

Russel finished his pizza and joined her in the living room, sitting on the opposite side of the couch, his eyes on the fire. "It was okay. More meetings. More chaos. You know."

Claire didn't know. She'd only been to New York City a handful of times.

"I take it you haven't heard from Gail?" Russel said. His voice was edged with worry.

In a weird way, just knowing he cared enough to ask was a relief.

"No," Claire said. "But Rina was able to access some of her messages. It looks like she had a boyfriend, after all."

Russel's shoulders loosened. He looked like he'd just won the lottery. "That's good news, right?"

"Why is it good news?"

"Because she's probably with this guy," Russel said. "I mean, that's normally what happens with these kids. They fall in love too quickly and make rash decisions. And then, when the relationship inevitably fails, they come home. Right?"

Claire pressed her lips together. On the one hand, Russel was right; even Rina had said over the phone that nine times out of ten, that was the case. But what about the tenth time? What if Gail fell under that horrific, ten-percent chance?

"It's been ten days, Russel," Claire said.

"Exactly. Ten days is nothing. It's a breeze. Remember when she read that Kerouac novel?"

"*On the Road?*"

Russel snapped his fingers. "She was obsessed with it. She always talked about going on a road trip across the continent. Remember? She and Abby had that whole plan."

"But they were going to do that after college," Claire protested. "And they weren't hiding it from us."

"Mark my words," Russel said. "That's what she's doing."

Claire's throat threatened to close up. She gaped at this man, this man she'd loved for decades, and blurted, "Why are you being so cold?"

Russel's smile fell, and his expression was suddenly stony, his cheekbones carved from rock. "I don't know what you think you're getting out of all this. Moping around the house isn't going to bring Gail back."

Claire sputtered. "Russel!"

Just as quickly, Russel changed his expression. His eyes softened, and he wet his lips. "I'm sorry," he said, ripping his fingers through his hair. "This is just as hard for me as it is for you. But I'm throwing myself into work. I'm trying to distract myself. When Gail wants to come back, she will."

"But what if she needs us, Russel? She's eighteen years old."

Russel was quiet. In the fireplace, a log crumbled, disintegrating into ash.

"I'm going to hire Rina," Claire said. "Officially."

Russel raised his shoulders. "You know what people do when they feel they're being chased?"

Claire didn't answer. Her heart thudded.

"They run faster," Russel went on. "You're going to drive her further away."

* * *

Russel went upstairs to shower the city off him. Claire remained in front of the fire, fuming, her blood pressure skyrocketing. She tried to imagine the father Russel once had been, the one who'd been there in the delivery room with her as Gail and Abby had joined them in the world. That version of Russel would have never been so blasé about one of their girls going missing.

Claire burst to her feet and stormed upstairs to rap on Abby's door. "Honey? We're going to Grandma and Grandpa's. Pack a bag. We're leaving in five."

Abby recognized the urgency in Claire's voice and jumped in the passenger seat of the van right on time. Her cheeks were flushed, and her hair was wild and mangy. "What's going on?" she asked as Claire backed out of the driveway. "Didn't Dad just get home?"

"Your grandmother wants to cook for us tonight," Claire lied.

Abby was quiet, watching the snow-lined trees, the houses they'd driven past thousands upon thousands of times, the twittering winter birds in the low-hanging branches.

"Mom?" Abby asked, her voice crackling. "Are you leaving Dad?"

"What?" Claire tried to make her voice high-pitched and friendly. "No."

But in her gut, another voice muttered a different answer. She just wasn't fully ready to acknowledge it yet.

Claire pulled into the driveway of the home she'd grown up in, cut the engine, and gazed up at the gorgeous home with its wraparound porch and sturdy oak in the front yard. When she'd married Russel, and when she'd opened the flower shop, she'd known she would never have the wealth her parents had. It now seemed staggering. So many rooms. So many zeros in the bank account. So much comfort in times of strife.

But all the money in the world wouldn't bring Gail back to her.

After they entered and hugged Kerry hello, Abby hurried upstairs to see Rachel. Claire collapsed in a kitchen chair and rubbed her temples. Her mother's warm arms wrapped around her, and Kerry burrowed her face in Claire's shoulder.

"I've been praying endlessly," Kerry whispered. "We need answers."

Charlotte appeared in the kitchen wearing a big T-shirt and a pair of exercise shorts. With her hair in a flipping ponytail, she looked nearly the way she had thirty years ago when they'd been teenagers. She joined the group hug with Kerry, and together, they held Claire together as though she were a broken pot that needed gluing back together.

A moment later, Andy appeared in the doorway of the kitchen. "Hey, sis." He smiled tentatively, and Claire burst to her feet to hug her baby brother. For so many years, he'd been missing, too.

"What are you doing here? Shouldn't you be at work?" Claire asked, sniffing. Andy smelled like the woodworking shop he worked in, where he refurbished antiques and built gorgeous wardrobes, desks, and even pianos. The pianos were his pride and joy, stylish and beautiful—but most people didn't require new pianos these days.

"I got the rest of the day off," Andy said. "Dad and I are playing chess. He's killing me."

"I'll make up a plate of snacks," Kerry said. "And we can gather in the living room. There's a great documentary on right now."

"Let me guess," Charlotte said. "It's about World War II?"

Both Kerry and Trevor were World War II buffs. They'd seen every film and documentary and read nearly every book on the subject. Claire had once suggested that Kerry write her own book based in the forties. To this, Kerry had said, "I don't need to contribute. I'm no artist. I just love learning as much as I can."

During the war, both of Kerry's parents had been in Martha's Vineyard. They'd fallen in love at the Aquinnah Cliffside Overlook Hotel as the war had raged on in Europe.

"Here's a surprise," Claire's father said as Claire entered the living room. Trevor was stationed in front of the chessboard, with one eye on the World War II documentary and another on Andy's next movements. She dropped down to give him a hug. She was swaddled in the warmth of her family.

"Maybe I can steal Kelli from the Aquinnah Cliffside Overlook today," Kerry said, tapping her lip. "It would be nice to have everyone under one roof."

"Steve's off gallivanting through California," Trevor said as he tapped a bishop into place.

"Have you talked to him?" Charlotte asked, sitting cross-legged on the floor beside her mother's chair.

"This morning," Trevor said. "He said he's got a tan."

"And what did he say about Rina?" Kerry asked.

"I asked," Trevor said. "But only because you told me to, my love."

Kerry rolled her eyes. "And what did he say?"

"He said they were very good friends," Trevor said.

Everyone in the living room groaned.

"Is that all?" Kerry asked.

"He said there was some confusion between them," Trevor went on, "about what they were or could be to one another. But they've talked. And they're going to remain friends."

Again, everyone groaned. Claire felt herself giggle just the slightest bit. It felt nice to care about something so trivial.

"And what did you say?" Kerry asked.

"I told him I understood," Trevor said. "Laura hasn't been gone long. And it's important to grieve."

"That's wise, Dad," Charlotte offered.

"But that doesn't mean I don't think he should find love eventually," Trevor added, adjusting his spectacles. "Having a life partner is a beautiful thing. It's stabilizing." He eyed his children one after another— first Andy, then

Charlotte, then Claire. "I'm thrilled all of you have found wonderful partners. Charlotte, I'm guessing I'll weep like a little baby at your wedding to Everett."

Charlotte laughed into her hand as Claire's stomach did a somersault. Again, her gut spoke to her. This time, it said: Dad doesn't know the real Russel. Not anymore.

"One final thing Steve said," Trevor added, returning his attention to Claire. "Apparently, Rina is digging more into this Nathan Rodgers fellow. Steve says she can't resist a case. And more than that, she apparently fell in love with the Montgomery clan during her time here. She wants to help."

"That's wonderful," Claire whispered. A wave of emotion crashed into her chest.

"It's perfect," Charlotte agreed. She reached up to tug on Claire's hand. "She's going to find him. She always does."

"We'll have our Gail back in no time," Trevor said.

The family was quiet for a moment, imagining Rina out there, hot on Nathan Rodgers's heels. Although Claire didn't know what he even looked like, she'd begun to insert various features of men she knew from films. He had Jake Gyllenhaal's face and Jeremy Allen White's hair; he had the body of George Clooney and the voice of Bradley Cooper. And if he was really responsible for taking Gail away, Claire was unafraid to punch him directly in his perfect nose.

"Rina didn't just fall in love with the Montgomery family if you ask me," Kerry said under her breath, interrupting Claire's reverie. "Didn't you see the way she looked at Steve? A mother knows when someone loves her son. A mother always knows."

Chapter Sixteen

ent on taking back control of a life so completely off-kilter, Rina insisted on driving Steve's rental back home from the restaurant. Her knuckles were bright white as she shot them out of the parking lot, driving twenty miles over the speed limit, whizzing through the California dark. Steve was quiet beside her, gripping his knees with terror. He knew better than to say anything, not now, as Rina's mouth tasted of pennies, and her heart dropped into her stomach. When Rina pulled into a parking lot not far from the restaurant and bucked out, he followed her.

Rina felt out of her mind. She tore into the dive bar called The Rusty Nail, slammed herself on the nearest stool, and ordered two tequila shots from a bartender with an eye patch. She remembered him, impossibly, from thirty years ago, back when she and Cody had gotten into the bar with fake IDs and drunk two-dollar beers until he'd kicked them out. Back then, he'd had the eyepatch, too. It was his thing.

"Rina?" Steve's voice rang out behind her, but Rina

didn't turn around. She took both tequila shots, one after another, and rapped on the counter to order a beer.

Steve slid onto the stool beside her. He seemed to know not to touch her. Rina's chin quivered, and she bit her tongue to avoid bursting into tears.

"Can I get you something?" the bartender asked Steve.

"Just a beer," Steve said. "Thanks."

The bartender put both beers in front of them and fled the bar area, abandoning them to smoke a cigarette outside. Rina was too intense, even for the man with one eye.

"I can't imagine what you're feeling right now," Steve said.

Rina raised her shoulders and curled her fingers over the bar. She had half a mind to go outside and demand a cigarette. She hadn't smoked since the nineties, but desperate times called for desperate measures.

"He just came out with it," Rina rasped. "Just like that. Like it was nothing."

Steve was quiet. Rina didn't want him to think she was blaming him. After all, he'd done precisely what she'd asked him to. He'd played the part of her boyfriend so they could get information out of her father. And boy, had they gotten information.

"It was obviously something to him," Steve said quietly. "He kept it from your mother for a month, he said. It terrified him to know about her. He didn't know what to do."

Rina ground her molars together and took a big swig of beer. "They blamed me for her disappearance, you know. All those years. They told me it was my fault she was gone."

Steve's face was stony. After a long pause, he finally said, "From what you've explained to me, it sounds like your parents aren't good people, Rina."

The statement rang so true that it brought tears to Rina's eyes. She turned to face Steve fully. Just then, she wanted to drown in the tenderness he showed her. She suddenly felt as though nobody in the world had ever known her the way Steve did. As though, all these years, she'd been searching all over the world for missing people, and she'd been the one who was gone.

"She's just two hours away," Rina whispered. "All those years, I was looking for her. How did I not find her?"

Steve raised his shoulders. "She didn't want to be found."

"But why did she reach out to my father instead of me?" Rina blared. She smashed her fist on the countertop, and her hand stung. "I've been here. Like a lighthouse. Waiting to guide her home."

Suddenly, Steve took Rina into his arms, and Rina bawled into his chest. Her body shook violently, and she fell off the stool and stood in the warmth between Steve's legs. She was swallowed by him. She never wanted to step away from him. All she wanted was to inhale the salt of his skin and hear his beating heart, just on the other side of his ribs.

Back at the restaurant, as Rina had gaped at her father in stunned silence, Wally had said he hadn't yet seen Penny in the flesh. He'd wanted to wait to take Ellen with him. They'd only spoken on the phone once. When Zach had pressed Wally for details, asking where Penny had been all these years and why she left in the first place,

Wally had laughed and said, "I don't know! I was so excited that I forgot to ask."

"I'll go with you," Steve said quietly, wrapping his hand over Rina's head. "To see your sister."

Rina froze. She felt jagged, sharp, as though she couldn't trust anything she said not to be cruel. Suddenly, everything crumbled around her, and she snapped away from Steve and blinked up at him. The white shirt she'd bought him was a mess, stained with black eye makeup and red lipstick. His face was so handsome, like an East Coast James Dean, and she suddenly hated that he was here, that he pitied her so much. She regretted that she'd shown him so much of herself.

"No. You can't go with me," Rina blurted. "I don't even know why you're still here."

Steve hardly flinched. It was as though he'd sensed her mood change and was ready to accommodate it. This annoyed Rina even more.

Rina flattened a twenty-dollar bill on the counter and stormed back into the night. Steve rushed after her. There was nothing but the Pacific winds in her ears, the thick ache of the salty air. There was nothing but the moon, pregnant on the horizon, casting its glow on the frothing waves. Everything felt terrible, like a car accident you couldn't help but watch.

"Rina!"

Steve's voice was almost violent, and it stopped Rina in her tracks. She turned to glare at him. She was gripping the keys so hard that they'd nearly torn the skin of her palm.

"You don't understand," she called through the rushing winds. "And I can't explain it to you. Okay? We aren't in one another's lives. We aren't anything to each other. And I have to deal with this on my own. Just like I've dealt with everything else."

Steve stepped closer, and a wrinkle formed between his eyebrows. He looked confused, quizzical, on the verge of figuring out a crossword puzzle.

"Don't you get it, Rina? Don't you get why I'm here? Why I bailed on the auto shop? Why I left my family and friends back home?" he continued, his voice breaking. "I'm in love with you. I've been in love with you for months. And I haven't known what to do about it. I've been scared, so violently, achingly scared, that I haven't been able to say it aloud. And we've been living in that purgatory together—a purgatory I created. And I'm sorry, okay? I'm sorry I did that to us. But I want to start over. I want to try."

Rina gaped at him, struggling to breathe. She felt as though she'd just run ten miles.

"You don't have to lie," Rina rasped. "I'm having a bad day. So what? I've had bad days before. I'll deal with it. I don't need any heroic gestures."

Steve laughed, clearly exasperated, and placed his hands on his hips, like a cowboy. "As far as I can tell, you come from a horribly narcissistic, manipulative, selfish family. Your sister is included in that. You've never needed anyone but yourself. And that's fantastic. Really. It's a life skill that many don't have. But I want to be here with you. I want to help you through this. And I don't want to do it as your friend."

Rina pressed her hand over her stomach and tried to fill her lungs. The tequila shots rang through her, and the lights over the bar blurred.

"She was my best friend. I did everything for her," Rina muttered, thinking again of Penny—of her silly stories, the way her laughter rang through the halls at school, of how proud Rina had been of her when she'd won academic awards and been voted class president. Their parents hadn't cared a lick about Penny or Rina's achievements—and Rina had had to care doubly, for the both of them.

"You owe it to yourself to find out why," Steve said, stepping forward to take Rina's hand.

Rina nodded. It was exactly what she told so many of her clients, who were flabbergasted when their family members, friends, or lovers had spontaneously gone away. It was startling to be on the other side of that conversation.

Rina placed her hand on Steve's cheek and gazed into his eyes. A voice in her head told her not to; that it was too messy, but the tequila shots made her feel like honey, and she rose onto her tiptoes to kiss Steve's perfect lips, to close her eyes as the world spun around them. Steve's arms wrapped around her, and he lifted her against him, there in the terrible shadows of the dive bar parking lot. And for the first time since Penny's disappearance, Rina had the ridiculous sensation that everything would be okay.

"Shall we go back to your place?" Steve whispered as he returned her to solid ground.

Rina nodded. Her knees were jelly.

"You have to let me drive," Steve said, taking the keys from her hand.

"Control freak," Rina teased, punching his arm lightly.

"I should say the same to you."

Chapter Seventeen

Sunlight spilled through the bedroom window, illuminating the sheets that wrapped around Rina and Steve's ankles. Steve was still fast asleep, his broad chest filled with coarse chest hair rising and falling, his lips parted, and Rina propped herself up on her elbow and gazed at his profile in disbelief. For months, all she'd ached for, all she'd imagined was this— being with him in this very real yet simple way. But the beauty of it was staggering. Tears sprung to her eyes.

Rina tip-toed to the kitchen and brewed a pot of coffee. Standing in her sleeping shorts and a tank top, she listened to the bubble of the coffee pot and watched three sparrows' flit through her backyard. Several of her plants looked more vibrant than ever, the green of their leaves thickening.

In the wake of her father's big reveal about Penny, Rina had been a walking, talking mess. She'd ordered tequila shots like a frat boy on spring break; she'd driven like a maniac. And then, she'd thrown herself at Steve, beneath that ancient tapestry of stars over California. All this recklessness wasn't like her.

There was no telling what would happen when Steve woke up. She tried to imagine him ambling down the hallway, palming his neck. She could practically hear him, telling her that it had all been a mistake. That, or worse. Maybe he'd tell her he just wanted to distract her. Maybe he'd tell her it had been for her own good, but it was never happening again.

Rina checked her phone, hoping for a distraction. Instead, she found a text message from her father.

> WALLY: Hated to see you run out like that
> last night.

And after that, was a phone number. Rina's heart thudded. She knew it was Penny's.

But why had her father sent it? Rina racked her brain to understand this man; this horrible, selfish man. Images from long ago splintered her mind. There was her father on his sailboat, a cigar between his teeth, yelling at Rina to "tie the rope the way he'd taught her." Rina, crying, not sure what he meant. Penny with her hands over her ears, begging everyone to stop yelling. Her mother, drinking a cocktail and watching the waves as though nothing was wrong.

Rina didn't have the heart to call Penny on the phone. There was something so impersonal about it. That, and it was so easy to just hang up when things got uncomfortable. She imagined Penny's voice, yet aged up thirty years, and it sent a shiver down her spine.

Rina found her laptop in the next room and used one of her "semi-illegal" services to run Penny's cell phone number and find the associated address. Just as her father said, Penny was about an hour and a half up the coast, on the outskirts of Santa Barbara. If Rina wanted to, she could get in her car right now, drive up, and accost Penny over her morning coffee.

The hallway floorboards creaked, and Rina jumped up as Steve entered the living room, rubbing sleep from his eye. His smile was tender, nervous. Rina's heart flipped over. Silence filled the room like water gushing into an empty tank.

And then, Steve cleared the distance between them and kissed her on the lips. Rina's skin sizzled with electricity. When he pulled back, he gazed into her eyes and touched her cheek. He was doing everything you were meant to do when you were in love, Rina thought. But could she trust it?

"I made coffee," Rina said.

"Thank you." Steve retreated into the kitchen to pour himself a mug. He then sat on the couch directly next to Rina. He looked entranced with her. Rina placed her computer on the coffee table and clutched her mug with both hands. The awkwardness in her limbs made her feel like a teenager, unsure of her body.

Suddenly, Rina knew there was only one thing to say. One thing to seal what had happened between them.

"I'm in love with you, you know."

Steve's cheeks were blotchy and pink. "And I'm in love with you."

Rina's lips quivered into a smile. He'd come out West for her. He'd pushed through his grief for her. He wanted her in his life—for good.

"I would love to stay inside with you all day long," Rina whispered.

Steve shook his head ever so slightly. "But we can't."

"I can't," Rina agreed as her shoulders sagged. "I need to go see her."

More than that, she needed to understand. There was so much she couldn't wrap her mind around right now.

"But after that," Rina added, "after I rip the Band-Aid off this thirty-year-old wound, we're going back out East. Your sister needs us."

Steve set his jaw and reached for Rina's hand. "You're amazing. You know that?"

Rina showered and changed into a pair of loose jeans and a white T-shirt, added a touch of lipstick, and then removed the lipstick immediately, smearing the back of her hand across her lips. She could imagine Penny saying, "Why are you trying so hard? It's just me."

Rina and Steve filled to-go mugs with coffee and walked out to the car. Outside, there was a strange glow to everything, as though the sun was shining through a greenish film. Rina pressed on the gas and shot them out of her neighborhood toward the glinting Pacific. Driving by the water had always stabilized her. It reminded her of just how small she was, that she was just a single member of a planet upon which eight billion people lived. That meant she could handle anything.

Steve and Rina talked intermittently on the drive up to Penny's place. Rina's head was too full of fears for normal conversation. Steve flicked through radio stations, landing on classic rock songs by Led Zeppelin, Pink Floyd, and Gong. Rina pulsed her head in time to the music, trying to pump herself up.

"This is so unique," Rina said suddenly when they were just five minutes from Penny's place. "I mean, how many private investigators get to solve their oldest, coldest case?"

Steve squeezed her arm gently. "How many sisters get to reunite after thirty years?" He smiled. "But I've told you about the Sheridan sisters, haven't I? How they all left Martha's Vineyard, one after another, and didn't return for twenty-five years?"

"They act like they never spent a day apart."

But Rina couldn't help but point out the differences. Penny had actually "disappeared." She'd "gone missing." The Sheridans had looked one another in the eye and said, "I never want to see you again." There was more finality in that. There were more sleep-filled nights.

Penny's house on the coast was a mini-mansion, approximately ten times bigger than Rina's little place in Santa Monica. Rina's mouth was dry as she shut the engine off and gazed up at it to view it's glass walls and white pillars, and it's sharp angles. It spoke of modernity and fat bank accounts. The lawn that stretched around it was lush and as bright green as astroturf.

A long time ago, Penny and Rina had joked about people who cared so much about their lawns. It had seemed like the most mundane thing in the world.

"I'll wait in the car," Steve said. "Unless you want me to come with you? Then I'm there."

Rina felt rigid like her arms and legs were made of bark. "I'd better go alone. But thanks." She kissed Steve and stepped out from the car. Her heart pounded as she headed up the walkway. She felt as though she was walking toward her doom.

If Penny didn't answer, what would she do? Would she see it as a sign and give up?

Rina reached the front door and took a deep breath.

She was struck with another memory: she and Penny maybe forty years ago, playing hide-and-seek. Penny had been in the cupboard where they kept the cleaning supplies. Rina had known all the time where she was, but she played along for a while, pretending to look in corners and behind window curtains. When she finally reached the cupboard, she knocked on it, just like this. And Penny had squealed with laughter on the other side.

Rina rang the doorbell. The sound echoed through the glass house and spread out across the lawn. Rina glanced back at Steve, who gave her a firm nod. Whatever happened here, he would remain beside her. They had a future.

The door clicked open slowly. Rina turned back to find a middle-aged woman with long, highlighted hair, the blonde shimmering in the California sun. The face was layered with makeup, and the nose was different, smaller. A nose job, maybe. Penny's eyes were as wide as a Disney Princess's.

Normally, when Rina found who she was looking for, relief rushed over her arms and legs, and her lungs filled with air. But this time, it felt as though she'd been punched.

"Rina," Penny whispered.

Rina blinked at her little sister. She remembered herself, only days ago, touching the mural on the high school, aching to know where she was. She felt like a fool.

"Can I come in?" Rina asked.

Penny stepped aside and beckoned for Rina to enter. They were quiet as they walked down a long hallway, its walls glass, toward a back kitchen with Mexican tile. Penny asked Rina if she wanted a cup of coffee, but Rina refused it. Such normality didn't seem correct.

Finally, they sat in chairs by a turquoise swimming pool in the shape of a teardrop. California sunlight draped over their feet and ankles, but they were otherwise in shadow.

Rina burned with questions. None of them seemed right to start with. But it didn't matter, anyway, because soon, Penny spoke first. "I've imagined this moment for decades."

Rina was quiet. Maybe her silence would force Penny to say everything.

Penny leaned forward and touched her temples. Her blonde hair cured loosely down her back. Rina compared it to her own brown bob. She'd wanted it because it was the easiest thing to brush through in the morning. She'd wanted ease.

"Oh, Rina. Rina, Rina. I was so young," Penny said to the swimming pool. "Fifteen years old. And so brash. So confident. Sometimes, I think, if I could have bottled my personality back then, I could have made a lot of money."

Rina spoke then. "It seems like you do all right for yourself."

Penny's laughter was musical. Rina hated how much she loved to hear it.

"That's my husband," Penny said. "Joshua. I do odd jobs here and there, but he's the breadwinner. Always has been."

"Where does he think your family is?"

Penny rolled her head back, and the tendons in her neck cracked and popped. "I met Joshua when I was twenty-five. And I told him, well, I told him my parents were dead. To me, they were."

Rina's heartbeat intensified. "And your sister? Did you say your sister was dead, too?"

Penny shot Rina a look, and her smile fell. Rina had the urge to tell Penny how much she'd destroyed her. That, after Penny had disappeared, Rina had fallen into a tremendous depression that had lasted years. That she'd met and married a man who'd cheated on her and killed what little self-confidence she had left.

Penny had abandoned her. And Rina was the messy remains of that crime.

"Come on. You had to have known where I was," Penny shot.

Rina parted her lips with surprise. "I'm sorry?"

Penny whipped her hair around. "That guy! The one I met at that party. Ben? He was like nineteen or twenty at the time. And he swept me off my feet. I was crazy for him. When he suggested we get out of town, I couldn't say no. I was too worried about losing him. Besides, he knew how much I hated our parents." Penny narrowed her eyes. "Don't give me that look, Reen. You hated them just as much as I did. And they didn't care that much for us, either. Talk about 'family love.' We didn't have much of it."

Rina gaped at her. "But what about me?"

Penny winced but remained quiet. She didn't have a good answer.

"What about me, Penny?" Rina repeated. "You were my sister. My best friend. And just like that, you were gone." She snapped her fingers. "And our parents blamed me. I blamed me. Everyone was looking for you. They even painted a stupid mural on the high school in your memory."

Penny chuckled but abruptly stopped. The air between them was taut and difficult to breathe.

"I knew you, Rina," Penny said quietly. "I knew you

had this obsession with right and wrong. That the minute I reached out, you would tell Mom and Dad where I was."

"That's crazy," Rina spat.

"You would have forced me to come home," Penny said. "But I was done with them. Mom and Dad were cruel and manipulative. They never cared about us. And I knew I was better off on my own." She straightened her neck to add, "And I was. I am."

Rina gaped at Penny, remembering the thousands of sleepless nights, how she'd roamed through Santa Monica with Cody, calling Penny's name as though she were a dog who'd escaped the fence.

"Why did you reach out to Dad, then?" Rina demanded.

Penny sighed and stared glumly into the swimming pool. "I have kids," she said simply. "And I got to thinking about them. What if they ever left? It tore me apart inside. And in a moment of weakness, I reached out to Dad. I always liked him more than Mom. He could be charming when he wanted to be."

Rina's heart pounded. One question burned through her mind. Why hadn't Penny reached out to her? Why hadn't she followed her guilt to calling Rina on the phone —rather than their father?

Penny wet her lips. "I just couldn't reach out to you first, okay? It was too heavy." She stuttered. "I felt too guilty."

Rina blinked back tears. She spun between wanting to shove Penny in the pool, hug her, or storm out of there. Could she do some combination of all three?

"Look, I know, it's a mess." Penny touched the corner

of her eye to collect a tear on the tip of her finger. "But it's the truth. In all its messy glory."

Rina searched for an apology somewhere in Penny's words, but she found none. She stood abruptly and staggered back toward the house. She needed to get out of there.

"Rina," Penny called, chasing her.

Rina broke into a run down the glass hallway and past the ornate pots and the expensive modern art. She passed photographs of children at various ages—a boy and a girl, it looked like. Rina had ached for children of her own. She'd tried tirelessly until Vic had left. Why had Penny been allowed that gift when Rina had been left all alone?

But when Rina reached the front door of Penny's horrible mansion, she opened it to find Steve waiting for her in the front seat of her car. Warmth flooded her chest.

"Rina," Penny said again, gasping. She was directly behind her in the foyer. Her forehead glinted with sweat. "I really am sorry."

There it was, the apology Rina so craved. It rang hollow.

"You broke my heart," Rina said, her voice cracking. "I've looked for you for thirty years, and you were always just up the coast. I will never make sense of that."

Penny scrunched up her face into a tight, red ball. "I hate myself right now, Rina. I really do."

Rina took several deep breaths. She tried to link this blond, small-nosed Santa Barbara resident with her curly-haired, giggly little sister, but she just couldn't. They were too far apart.

"Maybe we could meet again," Penny offered, tucking her hair behind her ear. "Maybe we could talk. Really talk. When we've both calmed down."

Rina closed her eyes. She wondered if Penny was manipulating her like their parents had so long ago? She couldn't make sense of it.

"I have to think," Rina said, turning away and stepping out the door. "Goodbye, Penny."

Chapter Eighteen

After she got the text from Steve, Claire waited at the window like a golden retriever, watching her neighbors' cars crawl past. Snow was as thick as icing across the windowpane, glinting in the January afternoon. Upstairs, Abby was giving an online presentation to her classmates, and Claire could feel the vibrations of her voice through the house. Somehow, Abby kept going, even as Claire felt herself disintegrating by the minute.

Steve's truck pulled into the driveway a few minutes later. After he shut off the engine, he and Rina spoke for a few minutes, Rina touching her brunette bob. Claire's heart surged. This was the woman who would bring her Gail back home. She was putting all her trust in her. Since they'd told her yesterday they were coming across the continent to help her, Claire had scoured the internet, reading stories in which Rina had been responsible for reuniting families. If she'd done such remarkable work for them, why wouldn't that luck extend to Claire?

As Rina and Steve ambled up the front walk, Claire

bucked to the foyer and opened the door. All at once, Steve's strong arms were around her. "Welcome back," Claire heard herself cry. "I'm sorry you had to leave the California sunshine for this."

Rina hugged her, too. "I needed a break from California. There's nowhere else I'd rather be."

Claire poured them coffee and asked them strained questions about their flight and about Rina's mother's health.

"She's doing better every day," Rina explained.

"What happened?" Claire asked.

A wave of sorrow passed over Rina's face. "My mother and father had an argument on a staircase. My mother smacked my father on the arm and lost her balance."

Claire's jaw dropped.

"I know what you're thinking," Rina hurried to say. "And no. I genuinely don't believe my father pushed her. Those two are thick as thieves. They always have been. For better or for worse."

Not long after that, Steve headed out to check on things at the auto shop. This left Claire and Rina alone in the kitchen as the house creaked against the winter winds. Rina took out a notebook and clicked the end of her pen. Claire understood it was time to tell her as much as she could.

"Steve said you need any information that comes to mind," Claire said.

"From you, Abby, and Russel," Rina affirmed.

Claire sighed and rubbed her neck. "That's the thing. I wouldn't talk to Russel if I were you."

Rina's eyes lit up. "And why not?"

Claire felt as though she was living in a nightmare.

"Apparently, Abby and Gail fought about Russel. Gail suggested Russel wasn't who we thought he was, and Abby got angry about it and refused to listen."

Rina clicked the end of her pen again and then scribbled something on her notepad. Her handwriting made Claire delirious to look at; it was only a scrawl.

"But you said Gail's disappearance probably has something to do with Nathan Rodgers, right?" Claire hurried to ask. "I mean, nine times out of ten, young people run away with their romantic partners. Right?"

"We can't rule anything out," Rina said quietly. "And if Abby indicates this was a topic right before Gail left, we have to take it seriously."

Claire's heart dropped. She took a long sip of coffee. "Have you found any sign of Nathan Rodgers?"

"Unfortunately, whoever this Nathan guy is, he's very careful about his internet presence," Rina said. "He moved out of his off-campus house toward the end of the year, but his roommates have no idea where he went. When my associate asked about Gail, the ex-roommates said she used to hang around there quite often. They hadn't seen her since the beginning of December or so."

"Which makes sense," Claire hurried to add. "Because she was studying for finals. She was writing papers."

"Maybe," Rina said. She eyed the ceiling. "Do you mind if I go upstairs and chat with Abby for a while?"

"Of course not," Claire said. "Her class should be over by now."

Rina padded upstairs gently, leaving Claire alone in the kitchen. She checked her phone for a text from Russel in the city, but there was nothing.

A split second later, a text came in from Steve. It was as though he knew she needed it.

> STEVE: Sorry I left so quickly. The auto shop is a mess.

> STEVE: How are things with Rina?

> CLAIRE: She already interviewed me. She's upstairs with Abby.

> CLAIRE: She seems to have her head on straight about this. But I can't help but think Gail is too far away to find.

> STEVE: She isn't, Claire. We will find her.

Claire didn't want Steve to leave her alone, even in texting. She racked her mind for something else to say.

> CLAIRE: How was California, anyway?

> CLAIRE: You look good. Healthy.

> STEVE: Let's just say Rina and I cleared some things up.

> STEVE: I'll explain in person.

> STEVE: But I can't believe she's been so patient with me. She's a saint.

> CLAIRE: She knows how special you are. We all do. I hope we show it.

Chapter Nineteen

R ina swallowed both Abby and Claire in hugs and stepped back into the staggering chill of the early evening. Steve's house was just a few blocks away, and she touched the house keys he'd given her, which hung loosely in her pocket, a reminder of all she'd gained. As she walked along the driveway, Charlotte pulled up with Rachel in the front seat. They waved frantically and popped out to hug Rina goodbye.

"We're staying the night," Charlotte explained, her head tilted toward the house.

"Do you really think Uncle Russel had something to do with this?" Rachel asked in a small voice.

Rina knew better than to promise or assume anything. "I'm going to do everything in my power to find Gail," she said. "And I'm taking what Abby said very seriously."

Rachel and Charlotte fled past her, toward the crackling fire and the soup Claire was making on the stovetop. This left Rina alone on the sidewalk, her hands shoved deep in her pockets as the winter wind cut her like shrapnel. She was thousands of miles from California, from the whimsical colors of Santa Monica Beach, from the peach sand, from the taco truck. Yet she couldn't shake the feeling she was where she belonged.

After she'd left Penny's place yesterday, Rina and Steve had driven all over the West Coast, listening to the radio and going over everything Penny had told Rina during their brief exchange. Ultimately, Steve had said something that stuck to her bones. "Your sister is just as selfish as your parents are. She wanted to protect herself from them. You got the full brunt of their personalities, the full weight of their attacks. And it's up to you if you want to forgive Penny for leaving you like that."

Rina still wasn't sure. Upstairs with Abby, she'd seen herself instead, cross-legged on the bedspread, telling the cops everything she remembered from the final day she'd seen Penny before she'd disappeared. Abby's eyes reflected her fear and shock, but they were also resigned in a way. As though she'd begun to recognize this new, Gail-free reality as her only one.

When Rina reached Steve's place, she was pleased to find Isabella in the kitchen, boiling a pot of water for pasta and slicing tomatoes. Isabella put her knife to the side, dried her arms, and hurried across the kitchen to hug Rina hello.

"My dad told me he's in love with you," Isabella said softly as she stepped away, still gripping Rina's arms. "And I said, 'duh.'"

Rina blinked away tears. She hadn't realized how much she'd wanted Isabella's approval until she'd had it. She treasured it as though it were a precious, breakable thing.

Rina poured herself a glass of wine and headed up to the office she used when she spent time here. There, she logged into her various accounts and reached out to her associates. She needed as many people as possible to needle through the events of Russel's life. It was as though Russel's decisions and movements were pieces of trash in a garbage can—and it all needed to be removed and identified as they hunted for clues.

The many parallels between Penny's and Gail's disappearance were not lost on Rina. Gail was upset about her father; she'd fallen in love with an older guy. She'd abandoned her sister and best friend without another word.

If Gail had left of her own accord, Rina forgave her instantly. She was naive. She was young. She couldn't possibly understand the weight of her actions.

Then again, Penny had been three years younger than Gail at the time of her disappearance. Why, then, was Rina so quick to forgive Gail and so willing to hold on to her anger toward Penny?

It was too personal, she guessed. She held the darkness next to her heart.

After Rina set the wheels in motion to hunt down Russel's movements, Isabella called from downstairs. It was time for dinner. Rina returned downstairs to find Steve showered and dressed in jeans and a T-shirt, showing Isabella photographs from his trip out West.

"Look at that shirt you're wearing," Isabella said, referring to the one Rina had bought him. The one she'd ruined with her tears. "You look like a guy who just got off a surfboard."

Steve beamed and chuckled. "Did you hear that, Rina? I looked the part."

"You can take the man out of the East Coast, but you

can't take the East Coast out of the man," Rina teased, rising on her tiptoes to kiss him.

Rhett arrived a few minutes later, stomping his boots of snow. The four of them gathered at the dining room table as the light outside dimmed to gray-blue. Rina wrapped spaghetti around her fork and ate heartily, even asking for second helpings, as Isabella and Rhett updated her and Steve about everything that had happened since they'd left the island. Apparently, everyone was up in arms about Gail's disappearance, sending photographs to friends across the continent and telling them to keep their eyes peeled for her.

"Have you ever worked a case for people you know?" Isabella asked Rina tentatively.

Rina swallowed, remembering how Penny had looked at her by the pool. She'd been a stranger.

"Sort of," she said. "My sister disappeared when I was a teenager."

Just like that, she dropped her single-biggest trauma at the table for all to hear. It surprised her how little it hurt to say aloud.

Isabella was taken aback. She touched her chest.

"Did you ever find her?" Rhett asked.

Rina nodded, and her cheek twitched.

"And she was okay?" Isabella breathed.

"She was." Rina's voice cracked. "But before I found her, I hadn't realized how much trauma and guilt I was carrying around because of it. I want to save Abby and Claire from that if I can. It's the worst form of torture."

Isabella and Rhett nodded solemnly. Under the table, Steve touched Rina's leg, and Rina wrapped her hand around his tightly, clinging to him as though she was about to float away.

After dinner, Rina retreated back upstairs to check on the status of Russel's case. It had only been an hour and a half since she'd kicked everything into motion, so she wasn't expecting anything. Not yet.

But what she'd downloaded thus far made her understand something: Russel wasn't an ordinary man. Russel was brash. He was selfish. And he was doing everything out in the open, almost as though he wanted to get caught.

Of Russel, her associate had written:

Russel accepted a property development job in New York City a little more than a year ago. The new job offered him four times the yearly salary of his gig on Martha's Vineyard. The only stipulation was that he had to make frequent trips into the city to meet with clients.

Already that first month, based on information from his hotel stays, Russel pushed his stays longer than his job required. He frequently called the hotel front desk to extend his room as though he didn't want to go home.

One month after Russel accepted the position, he opened a new bank account in the city under only his name— without giving his wife access. It's probable that his wife had no idea about the account. It is unclear what pushed Russel to open the account in the first place. Perhaps he fell in love with city life? Perhaps he already wanted to set the stage to leave?

From that day forward, he deposited one half of his earnings in the city account and one half into his family account.

Six months after Russel took the position in the city, he began looking for a new apartment there. He looked at ten apartments before deciding on a two-bedroom in the Upper West Side. Based on a brief correspondence with the real estate agent, it seems Russel wasn't alone during these apartment searches. CCTV footage shows that he was with a younger woman at the time. More CCTV footage taken from the final address of his new apartment shows them coming and going numerous times, hand in hand.

There's no name for the woman on the lease. However, a quick reverse-image search showed that the young woman's name is Caitlin Gregory. Her Instagram link is below. Crazily, Caitlin's Instagram isn't private, and it's filled with images of Russel. It's almost like they wanted to get caught.

Rina clicked on the Instagram link, her heartbeat pounding in her ears. A moment later, she was struck with images of a beautiful, early-thirties Caitlin, dressed in a long, sleek camel coat, arm-in-arm with her dapper, older boyfriend. Russel looked confident and happy. His hair was as thick as a healthy horse's mane and just as shiny, and he wore a sleek black peacoat that reeked of money— the kind of thing you couldn't get away with wearing on Martha's Vineyard. The kind of thing people would gossip about. "Doesn't Russel think he's someone special? What's gotten into him?"

Rina tore through Caitlin's social media account for a while, going back nearly a year, when Russel first popped into her life. It wasn't clear how they'd met each other, but there were ways, Rina knew. Dating apps. Bars. Russel had insane amounts of freedom in the city. He'd been allowed to visualize a new life for himself—a new version of himself, with heaps of cash and a brand-new girlfriend.

Penny and Gail had visualized new lives for themselves, too. And they'd gone for them, just as Russel had.

When Rina scrolled back to the top of Caitlin's Instagram, she realized she'd completely skipped over the most recent photograph. It featured Caitlin, alone, leaning against a brick wall with both of her hands over her stomach. It was rotund. Pregnant. Rina's heartbeat quickened. She clicked and read the caption, which said simply: "We're over the moon. Coming 2024."

Rina knew the "we" meant Russel and Caitlin.

Rina collapsed against the back of the chair, reeling. Claire's face floated in her mind. Those glistening, tear-filled eyes, the bags beneath them that proved she hadn't slept well in weeks. All the while, Russel was gallivanting through his new city life with Caitlin.

Rina had no idea how she would tell Claire the truth.

But more than that, she wasn't sure how this newfound information would help her scout down Gail. It seemed clear Gail had learned about Russel's second life. It echoed in what she'd told Abby. "Dad isn't who you think he is." But to what corners of the world had Gail run in the wake of that discovery?

Rina tiptoed downstairs to find Steve and Isabella in front of the television. They were watching a nature documentary and eating ice cream.

"Steve? Can I talk to you about something?" Rina's voice was like a string.

Steve followed Rina upstairs to her computer. Rina decided it was easiest to explain with Caitlin's Instagram, and she watched as he scrolled through the images—Russel and Caitlin eating brunch; Russel and Caitlin kissing at Washington Square Park; Russel and Caitlin moving into their new apartment, dangling the keys in front of the door.

All the color drained from Steve's face. His eyes,

however, were dry. The lines around his mouth were etched with rage.

"I'm sorry," Rina stuttered. She hated destroying the Montgomerys like this.

"No. It's good that you found this." Steve tugged at the collar of his shirt and then scrambled for his phone in his pocket. Without another word, he called Claire, who answered on the second ring. "Hey, sis," he began. His voice was nurturing. "You said Russel's not coming back till tomorrow?"

Rina couldn't hear Claire's responses.

"Okay. Listen. You can't let him stay at the house anymore." Steve said it as though he were translating facts about the weather. "You should text him. Tell him to come tomorrow and get his things. You should be at Mom and Dad's when this happens."

Rina's heart dropped. Although she tried not to, she couldn't stop thinking of her own divorce. When Vic had moved his things out of their house, she'd felt like a ghost, haunting the halls of a place she'd wanted to fill with children.

"We'll come over tonight and explain everything," Steve said.

Over the line, Rina could hear Claire growing increasingly frantic. Steve's cryptic words had only freaked her out more.

"Don't worry, sis," Steve assured her. "We won't let you go through this alone."

Chapter Twenty

Island weather was always changing. "Never trust the weatherman," Claire's father had always told her growing up. "He doesn't know his feet from his hands." And over the years, she'd found this to be true. Days meant to be rainy were often blisteringly sunny. Blizzards often gave way to gorgeous skies. After all, Martha's Vineyard was just a rock in the middle of the ocean. That meant they were at the mercy of outside forces. They were just along for the ride.

Claire sat in the sunroom of her parents' place, wrapped up in a blanket, watching as rain pattered against the panes. Their recent twenty-degree temperatures had suddenly skyrocketed to the fifties, which gave the air a strange, balmy feeling. It didn't suit January. But then again, nothing about 2024 had felt right. It wouldn't have surprised Claire to wake up and realize it had all been a nightmare.

Last night, Steve and Rina had told her about Russel's other life. Claire had fit the information seamlessly into her current knowledge of Russel: that he'd lost weight;

that he dressed better; that he never touched her anymore. It made sense.

Strangely, news of his relationship with Caitlin hadn't hurt as much as the money. He'd been privately keeping half of his income away from Gail and Abby. He'd talked at length about what they could "feasibly" offer their daughters when they went away to college. All the while, he'd been buying twenty-dollar cocktails at bars across Manhattan.

It was one thing to fall out of love with Claire. It was another thing entirely to fall out of love with their daughters. Claire's rage swirled in her stomach.

There was a creak in the hallway. Claire flinched and turned to find her father hovering in the doorway to the sunroom. He wore an old university sweatshirt with a small stain on it, and his hair was tousled. Claire hated to see the pity in his eyes. She figured she would have to get used to it.

"Your mother just texted," he said. "Russel's home."

Claire's stomach seized, and she thought she would throw up.

"Okay. Thanks."

Kerry had decided to park outside Russel and Claire's house to make sure Russel returned to get his stuff. "I want to know where he is at all times on this island," she'd blared angrily. "And I don't want him coming near my Claire or my Abby." Kerry had half a mind to demand the keys to the place after he left, too. But Claire reminded her that legally, the house was in his name, too. They couldn't just take the keys away. They had to hope he respected their wishes and left the island for the time being. Besides, he had a baby coming back in the city. He was needed.

Trevor entered the sunroom and sat on the couch beside Claire. He cleared his throat and followed Claire's gaze out the window, where a gray and angry wave tried to swallow the dock.

"I hope your mother doesn't kill him," he tried to joke. "We can't afford a murder trial."

Claire didn't have the energy to laugh. She shifted her weight.

Trevor's hands were in fists. He looked at a loss. "Do you think Russel had a hand in Gail's disappearance?" He asked. "Steve said Rina doesn't think so. But I just don't know. I want to go over there and demand answers."

"I don't know, Dad," Claire breathed. "Rina said if she finds any clues, she'll have him arrested for questioning. But right now, there's nothing."

Trevor locked eyes with her. "What does your gut tell you?"

Claire's mouth was dry. "I don't think he had anything to do with it."

Trevor's eyes glinted with tears. Claire understood. It was easier to put the blame on Russel. The alternative was just more confusion.

"He's been too distracted in the city to care what goes on with Gail," Claire said. "It would have taken too much of his energy to deal with her."

Besides, she thought. Russel was selfish and manipulative. But he wasn't an all-out monster. She had to believe that. Otherwise, she would go insane.

"Steve said Rina's off to Amherst today," Trevor went on.

Claire nodded. "She wants to dig around and ask questions about Nathan. She still thinks he's our best bet for finding her. I have to trust her instincts."

They were all Claire had left.

Trevor touched Claire's shoulder gently. Claire suddenly felt like a young, little girl talking to her father in their sunroom. She wanted to lean on him. She wanted him to take away all the pain in her heart.

"Dad?" Claire rasped. "Was he always like this? Were my instincts all wrong?"

Trevor's face was stony. "Russel wasn't always like this, no. He changed. I can't put my finger on when. But I guess I noticed it about a year or two ago."

"It should be illegal to change so drastically," Claire tried to joke. "I thought we were going to grow old together. We were so excited about the girls going off to college. We talked about traveling together. We talked about all the experiences we wanted to share."

But they were just pretty words, Claire saw now. Russel would have that other life with someone else. He would raise another child, maybe more. And maybe he would never look back on his life on Martha's Vineyard at all. Maybe nostalgia wouldn't get him down.

A few hours later, Kerry returned home. She looked frigid and volatile, and she put a kettle on the stove and paced the kitchen. Claire and Charlotte watched her from the kitchen table, waiting for her to pop.

"He loaded up several suitcases," Kerry announced. "And he drove back to the ferry." She stopped pacing and pointed at Claire. "But that doesn't mean I want you back in that house tonight. You're staying here. With us. Is that clear?"

Claire nodded. Charlotte squeezed her hand over the kitchen table.

"And I'm making my clam chowder," Kerry insisted. "Does anyone have a problem with that?"

Claire felt a smile play out across her lips despite everything. Her mother's anger was a powerful force guiding the Montgomery clan. She would have smacked Russel across the face if she had the chance.

As Kerry furiously sliced vegetables, there was a knock on the door. Charlotte answered it and brought Susan Sheridan in with her. Susan's eyes were lined with red.

"Claire, hi." She removed her coat and bent to hug her.

Claire remembered, abstractly, having reached out to Susan last night to demand an "immediate divorce from Russel."

"Another Montgomery divorce," Claire tried to joke, remembering how Susan had dealt with Kelli's a few years ago.

Susan waved her hand and took the chair between Claire and Charlotte. "I got divorced, too, remember. It's best to think of it as an escape hatch from a horrible situation." She wet her lips. "Remember, my husband left me for a younger woman, too."

Claire had forgotten that. Susan's first husband had even gone on to marry and have children with his mistress —his secretary at the firm where they'd worked together. Once upon a time, Claire had pitied Susan. But now, Susan was happier than ever with Scott. She'd begun again.

"I'll handle everything," Susan was saying of the divorce. "You have his work address? I can have the papers sent there."

"I do. Yes." Claire was amazed how wonderful it felt, watching people in her family take the reins on putting her life back together again.

"I'll strike a deal with his lawyer on the house," Susan said. "That and the flower shop will be in your name by the end of this. Mark my words."

Kerry demanded that Susan stay over for dinner. Susan couldn't refuse, not when clam chowder was on offer. Very soon, Claire felt herself sleepwalk to the dining room table, where she sat between Abby and Charlotte. The savory heat from the soup emanated through the air.

"Bless us, oh Lord," Kerry said, her eyes closed. "And bring our Gail back to us. We need her here. We love her so. Amen."

Chapter Twenty-One

Rina called Steve from a gas station parking lot in Amherst. It was terribly windy, and the rain careened sideways and splattered her face. After three rings, Isabella answered the auto shop phone and then fetched her father.

"Hey. How was the drive?" Steve sounded breathless. She imagined they were lying in bed next to one another, whispering in the dark.

"Uneventful," Rina said. "I'm about to meet with Nathan's ex-roommate. I don't have a lot of hope. But at least I'm digging around."

"Amherst has more answers than here, I'm afraid," Steve said.

"Have you heard from Claire?"

"Russel came and went this afternoon," Steve said. "My mother watched him like a hawk from the street."

"Atta girl."

Steve laughed gently. "Just be safe out there, okay? I want you back on Martha's Vineyard as soon as possible."

It was rare that somebody was so frank about needing

her. Rina had to steel herself from crying.

After they hung up, Rina paid for her gas and drove toward the outer banks of campus, where Nathan Rodgers had once lived with three roommates. After she knocked, a roommate with thick glasses and a band T-shirt opened the door, and a thick wall of body odor and pizza smashed into Rina's face.

"Wait here," the kid said. "I'll get Craig."

Rina waited in the foyer and assessed the living room: the television, the gaming devices, the *Pulp Fiction* movie poster, and the empty cans of beer. It looked like any typical college house. It wasn't hard to imagine Gail on the couch, eating chips and watching Nathan play video games. Rina had done similar things as a young woman, pining for the affection of older guys. She'd wasted so many hours on couches.

"You Rina?" A twentysomething guy came down the steps in his pajamas. It was only eight at night, and Rina guessed that he just hadn't gotten dressed today at all. He had very long arms and legs and a paunch, probably a result of all that pizza and beer.

"Hi, Craig." Rina shook his hand. "Thanks for meeting with me."

Craig indicated they could sit on the couch for the meeting. He ruffled his hair and looked at her coolly as though he was really high. It was possible he was.

"Have you heard anything from Nathan since he moved out?" Rina asked.

"Nope," Craig said. "But that isn't so weird for Nathan. He was never much of a texter. And we were friends, sure, but we weren't that close."

"Who was he closest to?"

"I don't know. He hung around that freshman girl a

lot. You mentioned her name on the phone."

"Gail."

"Right." Craig snapped his fingers.

"And you haven't seen Gail around at all since last semester?"

"Nope," Craig said, popping the p.

Rina felt as though she'd hit a brick wall. But she couldn't show weakness here, not to Craig. "Do you have any photographs of Nathan?"

"Oh. Yeah. I guess." Craig pulled his phone out of his pocket and began to flick through his saved photographs. It took forever. Based on what Rina could see from where she sat, Craig had taken a lot of photographs of graffiti. Maybe he drew it in his off-hours. But it seemed unlikely he had anything but off-hours.

"Here. These are from when we first moved in." Craig passed his phone over to show a photo of himself and three other guys. They stood on the front porch with their arms slung around each other's shoulders. Craig tapped his finger on the guy second to the left. "That's Nate."

Nathan Rodgers was slender, with black hair and a hint of black eyeliner, similar to the eyeliner Gail had been wearing on the night of New Year's Eve. He wore skinny black jeans and a big black T-shirt and didn't smile.

"Did he always dress like that?" Rina asked.

Craig shrugged. "He had his own style, sure."

"Are there any others?" Rina asked.

Craig flipped through the photographs from that first weekend they'd moved in. There were numerous porch shots, plus a few in the yard, where they'd set up a beer pong table.

"We were asking everyone to play with us as they walked by," Craig said proudly as though they were the life and soul of the Amherst party. "It got wild."

Rina studied each photograph, analyzing the sharp cut of Nathan's jawline for clues. In some of them, he was off to the side, leaning on a dark red Chevy. His beer was balanced on top of it as he lorded over the other beer pong players.

"Wait. Is that Nathan's car?"

Craig nodded. "Yep. That piece of crap was Nate's."

Rina's heartbeat quickened. She'd done a search on vehicles connected to Nathan Rodgers's name, but she hadn't found anything. She zoomed in on the license plate. Bingo. She memorized it immediately.

"Thanks so much for your help," Rina said, passing the phone back.

"Is Nate in trouble?" Craig asked.

"No. He hasn't done anything wrong. We just need to find him," Rina said with a smile.

"He isn't the kind of guy who likes to be found," Craig said cryptically. "He went off the grid all the time when we were friends. That's part of the reason we're not friends anymore, you know? You have to be able to rely on a guy."

Rina said she understood. She'd been surrounded by people she couldn't rely on her entire life. But they weren't her people anymore. She'd had to start anew.

* * *

Rina checked into the Hilton Hotel in Amherst, where parents normally stayed when visiting their children. The woman at the front desk assumed Rina was one of them; that she'd just had a wonderful reunion with her son or daughter on campus, celebrating all things academia.

"How are you enjoying Amherst?" she asked.

"It's wonderful," Rina lied. "My son couldn't be happier here."

Rina entered her hotel room, made herself some tea, and set her computer up on the thick mahogany desk. It was time to get to work. She had a target.

Nathan's license plate number continued to burn in her mind's eye. This was her longtime gift—photographic memory. She and Penny had experimented with it often during childhood. Penny had shown Rina a photograph for no longer than a second and then demanded Rina tell her everything she could about it. Rina's memory had amazed both of them.

Rina typed Nathan's number into a database, which she paid for access of, and watched as it spit out all relevant information tied to Nathan's car. Legally, it belonged to someone named Quinn Rodgers—a relative of some kind, maybe his mother. There were a few tickets associated with it over the years. Nathan had had a fender bender seven months ago in a McDonald's parking lot. None of it looked out of the ordinary.

But the most recent entry, Rina realized now, was from just six days ago. Nathan had been pulled over for speeding in Utah, of all places. Rina stood, and her chair toppled behind her. Utah. That was nearly a full continent away.

That was nearly all the way to California.

Rina suddenly felt jolted awake. Staggering back toward her coat, she rifled through the pockets to find her phone. Steve answered on the first ring.

"I can't believe I haven't thought about this," Rina gasped.

"What?" Steve sounded alert.

"On the night of New Year's Eve," Rina recalled, "I talked to Gail."

Steve sounded confused. "Did she say something?"

Rina could picture them plain as day: Rina, reeling after learning about her mother's accident; Gail, black-eyed, angry, smearing Rina's lipstick over her lips. Rina had mentioned she was going back to California. She'd even said where she'd grown up.

"I think she's going to Santa Monica," Rina whispered.

"To look for you?" Steve asked.

Rina blubbered with confusion. "I don't know." She explained what she'd learned so far: that Nathan had gotten a ticket in Utah. "I just have this gut feeling she's over there. It's as far away from all this nonsense as she could get. I can't explain it."

"You have to trust your gut feelings," Steve assured her. "When do you want to go? I'll meet you at the airport."

"Let me call Santa Monica police first," Rina said. "If they confirm, we'll leave in the morning."

"Call me when you know more."

Rina hung up, filled her lungs, and dialed the familiar number for Santa Monica police. It was the same station she and her parents had once entrusted to find Penny. They'd failed her once. That didn't mean they would fail her again. She hoped.

Before long, Rina was on the phone with an old friend of hers from high school, Cody's buddy, Jimmy. He was the same guy who'd brought the fireworks that night they'd nearly gotten arrested. Over the years, he'd been instrumental in handing over delicate information to Rina when she worked missing-persons cases. Although neither of them spoke to Cody anymore, they still liked to reminisce as though high school had been just a few weeks ago. Once, Jimmy had asked Rina out—but she'd said no.

"I was wondering if you could drive around to some of the cheaper motels in the area," Rina said. "I'm looking for a twenty-one-year-old guy and his eighteen-year-old girlfriend. They took off from the East Coast a couple of weeks back, and I have reason to suspect they're holed up somewhere in Santa Monica."

"Anything for you, Rina," Jimmy said. She could feel his smile through the phone. "By the way, I heard about your mother's fall. How is she doing?"

"She's healing up."

"Glad to hear it. The world is as it should be, then," Jimmy joked.

Rina paced the hotel room, switching from tea to wine to beer, waiting for Jimmy's call. It came just after eleven thirty, which was eight thirty California time.

"I found that car," he said. "And I saw a guy who fit your description coming in and out of the Sunset Motel to get something in the trunk of that vehicle."

Rina's heartbeat quickened. "But no sign of the girl?"

"Not tonight," he said.

"Can you do me a favor, Jimmy? Can you make sure they stay there?" Rina gasped into the receiver.

"This sounds serious. This guy isn't dangerous, is he, Rina?"

"I don't know," Rina answered. "I guess we'll find out tomorrow."

Chapter Twenty-Two

Rina and Steve grabbed the six o'clock flight from Boston to Los Angeles. Neither of them had slept more than a wink, and they guzzled coffee till their stomachs ached and held hands between the seats. When the plane touched down in California, it was nine thirty in the morning California time, and a cerulean-blue sky echoed above. Steve unzipped his winter coat and puffed out his cheeks. "So many changes in temperature in just a few days is giving me whiplash."

They'd packed lightly, just backpacks, which allowed them to breeze past baggage claim and jump into the first taxi. When the taxi driver tried to make small talk with them about "visiting California," Rina shut him down immediately and said, "I was born and raised here, sir." She felt like an exposed nerve. She just wanted to see Nathan Rodgers in front of her. She wanted to demand answers.

The taxi dropped them off at Rina's place, where they grabbed her car without bothering to go inside and drove the rest of the way to the Sunset Motel. True to his word,

Jimmy sat just a block away in his cop car, drinking coffee and eating a donut. He rolled down the window as they passed and waved the donut. "I'm upholding the old cop clichés, aren't I?"

"You're a godsend, Jimmy," Rina said. "Don't know what I would do without you."

"I haven't seen the guy since last night," Jimmy said, nodding toward the motel. "I imagine he's still asleep. The light was on till late." He tapped at his lips with a napkin, then added, "I'll stick around just in case, Rina."

The words "just in case" rang through the air between their cars. If Nathan was dangerous, that would open up a brand-new can of worms.

Rina parked in the motel lot and squeezed Steve's hand.

"I'm coming up there with you," Steve insisted.

Rina understood there was no arguing with him. She set her jaw. "Let me do the talking."

Rina and Steve headed up toward room 12, the door Jimmy had seen Nathan coming in and out of. Rina's heart pumped, and the ground beneath her seemed to tilt. Steve steadied her with a sturdy hand behind her back.

"You okay?" he breathed.

"Yes," she lied.

But Rina had begun to imagine Penny in that motel room—a teenage-version, waiting for Rina to find her. Lack of sleep was making her crazy.

Before Rina could chicken out, she rapped her knuckles against the door and waited, shifting her weight. There was a groan on the other side of the door, followed by a rhythm of words, two different sets of voices. Rina squeezed Steve's hand a final time and then released it.

"Hello?" A young man's scratchy voice addressed them from inside the room.

"Hi there," Rina said.

"We don't need you to clean the room or whatever," the man said.

"I'd like to talk to you for a moment, if I can," Rina said.

"Um. Why?"

Rina's throat was tight. "I'd like to ask you a few questions. Your name is Nathan Rodgers, correct?"

There was frantic muttering on the other side of the door. Rina couldn't make out anything that was said. Next came the creak of the bed and several small footfalls.

"What if I tell you to go away?" the man called back angrily. "What if I tell you I won't answer?"

Rina blinked back tears. "I don't want to get you in any trouble, Nathan. I just want to find Gail."

There was silence on the other side of the door. It was deafening. Rina's knees wiggled beneath her, threatening to give way. After that came a hiss from inside. Rina inhaled sharply as the two people inside the room—two people she prayed were Nathan and Gail—bickered quietly.

After a final growl, the door cracked open. A young woman with a clean, healthy face and long red hair peered out. Although she wore none of the black makeup from New Year's Eve, it was unmistakably Gail.

When she blinked out at Rina, she smiled, just as Penny had when Rina had discovered her during hide-and-seek. The jig was up. The game was over.

"Rina!" Gail said, opening the door wider. She looked

captivated. And then, her eyes flickered leftward. "Uncle Steve? What are you doing here?"

In the murky shadows behind Gail, Nathan sat on the bed shirtless, wearing only a pair of boxers. He was rolling a cigarette, and the bones of his shoulders were jagged, like those of a cheetah.

"I told you not to open the door," he said to Gail. He sounded bored.

Gail waved her hand in Nathan's direction. There was a strained silence. Rina tried to make sense of the previous two weeks of this young woman's life. She'd gone on a reckless adventure. She'd worried her mother sick. But she was all right. She was here, in one piece, at the Sunset Motel.

And based on the harrowing way she looked at Nathan now, she'd learned a very difficult lesson. She'd learned that pretty promises from young men didn't get you anywhere. She'd learned that abandoning everything you ever knew left you more alone than you ever thought possible.

Well. That was what Rina suspected, anyway. Maybe she was projecting.

"Let's go for a walk," Rina suggested.

"Don't go with them," Nathan shot out. "Or you'll never come back."

Under his breath, Steve urged, "Take your stuff."

Gail froze and locked eyes with her uncle. It had been weeks since she'd had a trusted adult around. It was as though all the cells on her body stood straight up, ready for instruction. It was difficult to be an adult and make every decision on your own without second opinions. It often felt like you were flailing through time without a sense of gravity.

Steve, now, was Gail's gravity. Steve was a reminder of the love of the Montgomery family, waiting for her at home.

Like a frightened rabbit, Gail hopped around the shadowed motel room, gathering her things and shoving them into a backpack. It looked as though she'd packed very little. That, or she'd lost things along the way.

"You're not going to just go," Nathan said, standing up as she neared the door. The bags under his eyes indicated he hadn't eaten a vegetable in years. Why were young people so cruel to themselves?

"Call me when you're back East," Gail said with a shrug.

"I told you. I'm not going back there," Nathan said. "What about surfing? What about our life?"

Gail seemed to take stock of him, her hand on the doorknob. Rina could practically feel the memories from the previous few months fly through her; she could feel the devastation of having thought he was someone or something he was not. That was the nature of dating as a young person. It meant trying and trying, having your heart broken, and trying again. It meant going to the ends of the earth with a person and realizing they weren't right for you. It meant learning and moving on.

"Just think about it," Nathan urged. "Go on your walk. I'll be here." He looked at her like a puppy in the window of a pet store, as though all he needed in the world was her love and care. It was difficult for anyone to walk away from someone as needy—especially someone as open to love as a teenage girl like Gail.

Gail stepped wordlessly into the California light, her backpack hanging loosely off one of her shoulders. Steve seemed to inspect every inch of her as though he expected to find bruises or broken bones. His lips were in a paper-thin line.

Rina drove Gail and Steve to Santa Monica Beach, where Gail asked in a small voice if she could talk to Rina alone. "Sorry, Uncle Steve," she said in the passenger seat, speaking to Steve, who was cooped up in the back with his knees close to his chest.

"Take all the time you need," Steve said.

Rina and Gail walked along the sands, gazing up at the Ferris wheel as it circled gently. The pastel colors of the morning had been burned away by the sunlight, and men and women were stationed along the beach, tanning, applying sunscreen, drinking green juices, and yawning lazily. It was hard not to fall into the dream of California. It was hard to remember that Martha's Vineyard beckoned so many states away.

"I fantasized that you would find me." Gail stopped short and crossed her arms over her chest. As she bit her coral lip, she looked far younger than her eighteen years; as though she were twelve, on the verge of a pre-teen breakdown. She'd wanted attention, and she'd gotten it. Just like Penny.

"Listen, Gail," Rina began, trying not to sound accusatory. "I know about your dad."

Gail closed her eyes. A seagull squawked overhead.

"Does Mom know?"

"She does," Rina said.

Gail covered her eyes with her palms and shook. It was as though all the stress of the previous few weeks fell upon her shoulder at once. Rina stepped toward her, weighing up whether or not she wanted a hug. Sometimes, in moments of such intense grief, touch was too intense.

"How did you find out about Caitlin?" Rina asked.

"I had a hunch about Dad over the summer," Gail said into her hands. "I was studying him like a book character, you know? He'd changed so much about himself. He'd dyed his hair. He dressed nicer. He whistled all the time. And, of course, he was hardly home."

"Did you tell anyone your suspicions?"

"I asked Abby what she thought," Gail said. "But she was so nervous about going to college. She couldn't see anything else but that. So, I decided to bide my time. To wait and see. And of course, college turned into this wild storm of newness. Abby and I were fighting for the first time ever."

"About Nathan?"

"Not just about Nathan," Gail went on. "About how messy the dorm room was. About what we were going to have for dinner. About what we wanted to watch on TV. It was crazy. Every time I looked at her, I saw my own face—but that face was fighting with me."

Rina clutched her elbows. "Did you think about asking to change rooms?"

"Abby would have never gone for it," Gail said. "And by the time I thought of it, I'd already met Nathan. I stayed at his place all the time." She let her hands drop. "Around Thanksgiving was when my suspicions for Dad grew even bigger. I talked to Nathan about it. About how done with my family I felt. And he suggested we leave as soon as 2024 began. It sounded so romantic to me." Gail's eyes glinted with the light off the Pacific. "We'd always talked about California. I barely knew anything about it. But our plan was to just head west and see what happened."

Rina had given her the name she'd needed: Santa Monica. And she'd leaped for it.

"You learned something else on New Year's Eve? Something that confirmed your suspicions?"

Gail nodded and kicked the sand. "I heard Dad on the phone. Mom and Abby were at the grocery store, and I think he thought I'd gone with them. Or he just didn't care anymore. He was talking to someone named Caitlin. He used the words 'divorce' and 'baby,' and I put two and two together." Gail scrunched her nose. "I saw red after that. And when Abby told me I was crazy, I went completely insane. I barely remember anything the week after that. Next thing I knew, I was getting into Nathan's car, and we were on the road. I didn't want anything to do with that life anymore. Gosh. I feel so dumb."

Rina let Gail's words hang in the air between them. It was hard to reckon with your own madness. Especially when you were only eighteen years old.

"Did Nathan hurt you?" Rina asked quietly. "On the drive? Did he pressure you in any way?"

Gail's eyes widened. "No," she said. "But I started having doubts not long after the trip began. I just didn't know how to turn back. I didn't know how to tell my mom I'd made a mistake."

Gail began to cry. Fat tears shimmered down her freckled cheeks, and her nostrils glistened. She needed a tissue. She needed her mother.

"Does she hate me?" Gail whispered.

Rina closed the distance between them and wrapped her arms around this young, foolish girl—a girl who'd learned far too much in the span of two weeks. A girl who just wanted to go home.

"Your mother could never hate you," she whispered. "She just wants you to come home."

And although Rina ached with the memory of what Penny had done, she felt closer to understanding her than ever. Penny had run too far and too fast. She'd gotten to the edge of a brand-new life and been unable to see her old one. The Penny Rina had once known was no more. And Rina had to mourn the old one—and start over with the new.

Chapter Twenty-Three

The phone call from Steve came just minutes after Claire re-entered her home for the first time as a separated wife. She opened the closets, the door of Russel's office, the fridge, and the spare bedroom, lost in years of memories, tumbling through images she couldn't return to. They'd brought their babies home here. They'd made love here. They'd built a life here.

"Hello?" Claire's voice was high-pitched.

"We found her." Steve sounded on the verge of tears.

Claire fell down on the kitchen tile. Her head spun. "You found her," she repeated as though daring him to take it back.

"She's here in California," Steve said. "We flew out this morning. I didn't want to tell you until we knew for sure. But I'm looking at her right now. She and Rina are talking on the beach."

Claire closed her eyes tightly, imagining her darling Gail in the sunlight, the salty breeze through her red hair. She was okay.

"She was with that guy," Steve said. "Nathan. But I get the sense things are ending between them."

"Does that mean she wants to come home?" Claire rasped.

"I don't know," Steve said. "The main thing, now, is we know she's safe. I'll keep you updated on our next steps."

"Oh, Steve. Oh gosh." Claire's eyes welled with tears, and she banged the kitchen floor with her fist.

"I know, sis. I do."

"I love you. I love her. I don't know what to say."

"We'll figure this out together," Steve promised her. "Just sit tight. She's coming back to the car. I'll call you later."

Claire curled up in a ball on the floor after that, listening as the wind outside burst against the house and whistled through the trees.

No mother should ever have to go through this, she thought. But she had. And she'd survived.

When she got the strength, she called Abby, who was still at her grandparents' house. When she told Abby what she knew, Abby burst into tears of shock. "I'm coming back right away," she said.

For the next few hours, Claire lived in fear that Gail would refuse to come home. She was an adult and could make a new life if she wanted to. She could cut all ties. Claire technically couldn't stop her.

Steve called that evening, announcing they'd gotten a hotel room in downtown Los Angeles for the night. Their flight was tomorrow. They would bring Gail home.

"Can I talk to her?" Claire asked, her voice heavy with tears.

"She's asleep," Steve said quietly.

"You didn't give her a room by herself, did you?" Claire was stricken. What if she snuck out?

"No," Steve assured her. "Rina's staying in her room. I have a room to myself."

* * *

Claire spent the following morning and afternoon doubled over with stomach aches yet determined to make the house feel "homey" enough for Gail's return. She and Abby scoured the grocery store for ingredients for lasagna, Gail's favorite dish, plus Gail's most-loved snacks, Twizzlers and Snickers and Sour Cream Ruffles and Blueberry Pop-Tarts. Their cart looked like a child's dream.

Back home, as she and Abby sliced vegetables for the lasagna, Abby paused and set down her knife. Her eyes looked far away and unfocused.

"I hope she forgives me," she whispered. "For not listening to her. For pushing her aside."

Claire gathered Abby in her arms and held her tightly. "You know what? I think you're already forgiven. The question is this. Do you forgive her for running away like that?"

"Not yet," Abby admitted, tugging her hair.

"It'll be a process for all of us," Claire admitted. "But we'll do it. Because there's no other option. And because we love each other to dickens. Don't we?"

Abby nodded and smiled for the first time in weeks. Claire wanted to bottle that smile and take it with her everywhere.

Steve's truck pulled into the driveway at seven-thirty that night. Claire whipped open the door and gazed through the blue night, watching as Rina opened the back door and handed Gail her backpack. Gail hopped out, her hair whipping out behind her. She hugged Rina with her eyes closed. Claire's heart somersaulted.

As Gail and Rina's hug broke, Gail stepped toward the house where she'd been raised, her eyes big enough to swallow the scene in one gulp.

And then, she spotted her mother. Abby hurried up behind her, peeking out from behind Claire's shoulder. For a moment, the three of them stared at one another in wonder, terrified about what awaited them after this.

Abby burst from behind Claire and ran along the walkway, her arms extended. Gail hurried forward, and the two of them burrowed against one another, weeping. Claire's heart shattered. Her girls were back together again. They'd found peace.

As Claire gathered her daughters back into the warmth of their family home, she waved through the darkness toward Rina and Steve, who held each other close in the front seat of Steve's car. Steve was crying, and Rina looked stoic and formal. They'd gone across the continent to find her girl. They'd brought her home.

That night, Claire, Gail, and Abby sat at the kitchen table and feasted on lasagna as another snow fell outside, peppering the island with white. Gail kept reaching for her mother's hand, bubbling with apologies. She asked for a second and a third helping of lasagna. And never once did her girls bring up the elephant in the room: they had to move forward without Russel. That he was officially gone.

But with Gail and Abby by her side, Claire was restored. Whatever awaited the three of them, they would face it with compassion. With awareness. And with each other. Forever.

Next in the Vineyard Series

Pre Order A Vineyard Celebration

Other Books by Katie Winters